WE WERE
SEEN

A psychological thriller with a great twist

MARK WEST

Published by The Book Folks

London, 2024

ISBN 978-1-80462-193-6

www.thebookfolks.com

For Stephen Bacon and Wayne Parkin

Chapter 1

The man stepped out of the shadows and blocked my way as I was going into the protest meeting.

"Councillor Morgan?" he asked.

He was tall and dark-haired, and I'd never seen him before.

"That's me." The vestibule of the Methodist Church Hall was narrow enough that I'd have to push past him if he didn't move. "Can I help you?"

"You're a difficult lady to pin down."

I don't know if it was his demeanour or how he'd positioned himself, but he made me feel slightly unsettled. "I'm not sure that's true, Mr..." I said and paused.

"Ogilvy." He held out his hand. "Simon Ogilvy."

"Kim Morgan," I said, and we shook. He had a firm grip. "I don't have a moment now, but I'd be happy to talk after the meeting."

"That would be excellent." His thin-lipped smile looked insincere. He moved closer and loomed over me. "My issue's all tied up with the same thing anyway."

"Is that so?" I said, determined not to be intimidated by his presence.

"Yes. I have an interest in the golf course proposal and wanted to talk through some elements of it with you." His smile widened and seemed less sincere.

My hackles rose at the thought of him trying to lobby me. "Are you in my ward or is this a more general approach?"

"The latter, Councillor Morgan." He chuckled. "But I'm sure you'll be open to speaking with me."

"I will. Now, if you'll excuse me?"

"Of course." He stepped aside and gestured for me to go by. "I'll see you later."

"I'm sure," I said and pushed through the door into the main hall.

The turnout was better than I'd expected. People milled around and the hum of conversation was loud. The gallery, around three sides of the room, seemed well-populated, too. The golf course proposal was something of a political hot potato locally, and it cheered me to think so many people took an interest.

Something caught my eye and I looked up to see my friend, colleague and ex-lover, Adam Wright, waving from the gallery. I waved back and, my attention distracted, walked into someone.

"I'm sorry." The man held my shoulder to keep me steady.

I quickly regained my balance. "No, it's my fault. I wasn't paying attention."

"You and me both."

He was about six foot tall and a couple of years younger than me. His white-blond hair fell attractively over his forehead and his piercing blue eyes seemed to dance with merriment. He had a strong jaw and a luscious mouth and reminded me of a Viking. He smiled and, for a moment, I was at a loss for words as a ripple of desire ran through me. Councillor at a public meeting or not, I'm a normal woman with human needs and if he'd asked me to go for a drink afterwards, I would have agreed straight away. I didn't, as a rule, often experience lust at first sight, but he was hot and I was very attracted.

He let go of me. "No harm done."

"As long as you're okay."

"Well," he said with a little laugh. "You knocked my shin, but I'm sure I'll live."

"It'd be a shame if not," I said and then caught myself. I was thirty years old, not some schoolgirl with a crush, and I had a job to do. I saw my friend Maureen over his

2

shoulder and waved to let her know I'd seen her. "I'm sorry, but I have to go."

"Okay."

I reluctantly left him and walked to Maureen who was leaning heavily on the banister for the balcony steps.

"Evening, love," she said, and we hugged quickly.

Maureen was in her late seventies, whip-thin and a couple of inches shorter than me at five foot five. She threw herself into projects that benefitted Seagrave without becoming a busybody, which is quite a trick to pull off. I liked and admired her and was delighted when she asked me to be involved with the protest group.

"You must be really pleased with this turnout," I said.

"I am, except I think it's because people are expecting a bunfight between me and Brian Glover."

"I'm sure that's not true," I said, without really believing it.

"Oh, I am." Her smile curled into a wince.

"Is everything okay?"

"No, my bionic knee isn't co-operating today. It hurts to stand and sitting isn't a whole lot better." She touched the back of my hand with fingers that were curled by arthritis. "Don't rush to get old, love. It's not what people tell you it'll be."

A stern-looking woman in her late sixties strode up carrying a clipboard. "Can you go to the stage, Councillor?" she asked, then looked at Maureen without waiting for me to reply. "I have a couple of questions, then you'll have to go, too."

Maureen raised her eyebrows at me, as if in defeat.

"I'll see you there," I said and made my way through the pews.

The stage was at the back of the hall. It was only a couple of feet high and covered less than half the width of the room. A pedestal lectern, wooden and old, had been set up at one end and a handful of seats were lined up alongside it. A banner, declaring 'No golf course, save our marshland', hung on the wall above the stage and the artist had included nesting birds in one corner while more birds flew over the letters.

"Well, it's certainly colourful."

The voice, close to my ear, startled me and I snapped my head round to see Brian Glover. He grinned. His teeth were very small and the colour of slightly off milk.

"I'm sorry, Councillor Morgan, did I make you jump?"

"Just a bit," I said with annoyance. "You shouldn't creep up on people like that."

"Creep up?" He smirked. "I hardly think that's the case." He rubbed his hands together briskly. "Are you ready to hear me tell people why my golf course project is essential for the well-being of Seagrave and its good citizens?"

He sounded more like a charming politician than a businessman. It was easy to see how people had been taken in by him. "I'm ready to hear you talk."

Glover shook his head slightly as if saddened by my response. "Why can't you accept it's a good thing after seeing my proposal and the statistics?"

"Because, Brian, we're both aware it's damaging to the environment and will be an elitist establishment."

"Elitist?" He said the word as if savouring how it felt in his mouth. "How so, Councillor?"

"You know your prices as well as I do." I had to be careful since I wasn't here representing the council and he knew that. Most of my colleagues felt a golf course and hotel complex would bring in much-needed tourism revenue as well as employment opportunities and couldn't understand my objections. Maybe they were swayed by Glover or hadn't read the literature, but I wasn't, and I had. He was going to build over marshland that should be protected and the hotel and course prices would be way out of reach of most people. "And that's not to mention the environmental destruction."

"A few newts or a few million quid? Hmmm." He patted his lip with his index finger. "That's a tough choice, isn't it?"

"It doesn't need to be."

He leaned in as if about to impart a secret. "Just because you think I'm wrong, it doesn't necessarily follow that you're right. It all depends on your point of view. Your precious marshes aren't protected, but I'm not a monster. I'm happy to throw in a little money to set up a sanctuary further up the coast to help your newts and nesting birds. Perhaps Sea Palling would be interested in taking something on?"

"You can't win everything by throwing money at it."

"Maybe not, but money makes the world go around and I have a lot of willing investors eager to fund the development of this site."

"And none of those funds will go to Seagrave or the people."

He gritted his teeth and I thought his smooth public persona was about to slip, but he took a breath then smiled smugly. He looked like a bully who knew he was going to get away with stealing my lunch money.

"I've been aware of the potential of that land for a long time and if anyone is going to make money from it, then why shouldn't it be me and my colleagues? I'm not some outsider, I grew up here and have as much right to the place as you. You, Maureen and your merry little band have put up a good fight, I admit that, but there can only be one winner and it's going to be me."

My temper was rising but then I saw Maureen struggling to get onto the stage. Glover and I both reached out to help her before he smiled and moved towards the lectern.

She looked at me. "Are you okay? You have some high colour in your cheeks."

"That's from talking to Glover."

"Ah," she said. "Property developers aren't renowned for being sensitive wallflowers, are they?"

Chapter 2

A microphone had been clipped to the lectern and Maureen tapped it gently, then asked for quiet. The audience, most of them pensioners, quickly complied. As she explained how the evening would run, I took the opportunity to look around.

Ogilvy leaned against the wall by the main door and a photographer who looked vaguely familiar moved between the pews to make his way down the aisle. The Viking was sitting near the back on his own and he'd clearly been watching me because when our eyes met he gave me a little wave.

I waved back and bit my lip to stifle a smile. Maybe it wasn't just me who'd been attracted and that felt nice. Since breaking up with Adam, my love-life had been quiet apart from two dates where I should have swiped left.

"It's really good to see so many of you here," said Maureen, "and your support is very much appreciated. The purpose of this meeting is to talk about the proposed golf course development and, while there are two distinct sides, I hope we can be civil." She smiled good-naturedly at Glover and he snapped off a quick salute. "Basically, this meeting is to listen to each side of the debate before the council votes on the planning this coming Thursday." She gestured towards me. "Kim Morgan is our ward councillor and also serves on the planning committee and we're very pleased she could join us. Sadly, no other councillors were available, but you can make your views known to them through emails, phone calls or social media." She leaned forward. "I'm sure they would all love to hear from you." There was a smattering of laughter. "And last, but not least, I'm happy to introduce Mr Brian Glover." There were a couple of half-hearted boos but they died quickly as if the people realised they were being rude.

Maureen's speech about the marshland and its overall importance was impassioned. She'd been a teacher and knew how to get her point across without feeling like she was beating you over the head.

She finished to a round of applause. The photographer had been taking pictures of her but now moved to get shots of the audience reacting.

"And now we'll hear from Mr Brian Glover."

He helped Maureen sit down then stood at the lectern. There were a few more half-hearted boos but they didn't last long.

"Thank you, ladies and gentlemen, for this chance to put my point across. I appreciate I might not change your mind but hopefully, by allowing me to explain the plans, you'll see that it's for the good of the local economy. After all, I'm a local lad done good, and I want to give something back to this wonderful community that raised me."

"And make a profit," said someone in the audience.

"Of course," said Glover without missing a beat, "for both the town and my company."

The main doors banged open and a group of men came through in a rush, talking loudly. I didn't recognise any of them and Ogilvy only moved his head to watch them go by.

Glover paused as if waiting for them to sit down but when they stood at the perimeter of the pews, he leaned towards the microphone. "If you'd like to take a seat, gentlemen, we're about halfway through the meeting. Unfortunately, you missed Maureen's excellent speech."

One of the newcomers stepped forward. His white T-shirt strained to contain his belly and his blue jeans had a crease in them. "We only wanted to hear you," he said and there was an edge in his voice I didn't like. He started walking down the aisle.

The other men spread out and there were at least ten of them. The atmosphere in the room shifted with that static charge you feel in a pub when you hear a light-hearted argument go up a pitch.

Glover nodded towards a broad-chested man I didn't recognise standing on the far side of the hall. "So, as I was saying…"

"Is that more lies?" asked the heckler. "Because that's all it'll be."

Maureen stood up slowly and held out her hands. "Excuse me, sir, but we're trying to have a civil meeting here."

The broad-chested man moved along the back row towards the newcomers, and it occurred to me he might be Glover's personal security.

"Don't make me laugh," scoffed the heckler. "He's going to try and con you like he does everyone else. He's not trying to help you, me or Seagrave. It's all about lining the pockets of him and his mates."

Glover's bodyguard followed the man in the white T-shirt down the aisle. The photographer, as if sensing something was about to kick off, angled himself beside the stage to better catch the action.

"Can I ask who you are?" Glover said.

"My name's Costigan. I'm born and bred in Seagrave."

"That makes two of us," said Glover. "It's a pleasure to meet you and if you're interested, I'd be happy to talk things through with you after the event. But right now, I'm delivering a speech to these good people."

"You're a swindler, Glover, and you're trying to con them." He glanced over his shoulder at the security guard. "And call off your attack dog. People have the right to know who you are."

Costigan made a dash for the stage.

I felt a jolt of surprise and looked at Maureen. She'd be hurt if she got knocked over, so I jumped out of my chair to put myself between her and Costigan. He leapt onto the stage and swung a fist at Glover that sailed wide of its target.

There were shouts and cries from the audience and I was aware of a struggle in the aisle.

"We need to stop this," Maureen said.

I held her shoulders. "We need to get you away from here."

She let me guide her away as Glover and Costigan circled one another warily. The security guard was fighting at least two of the thuggish newcomers in the aisle and a couple more were advancing on the stage. Some of the audience was leaving and people were coming down from the balcony and heading for the doors. The Viking came along the side aisle towards us, and I hoped he wasn't part of this mob. A couple of pensioners from the protest group climbed onto the stage as if to help Glover.

"Who are these men?" Maureen asked. She sounded surprised, sad and annoyed, all at once. "They'll ruin everything. I never wanted the protest to descend into this."

"I know." I helped her down from the edge of the stage.

Adam came down from the balcony and it was a relief to see a friendly face. "Come on," he said as he took Maureen's hand. "We need to get you both somewhere safe."

"Help her first," I said. "I'll be fine."

He started to protest but then helped Maureen to the stairs.

One of the thugs was coming towards me, looking like he intended to cause harm. He was on a parallel path to the Viking and fear made my mind race. I felt trapped and sweat trickled down my back.

The Viking put himself between me and the thug. "Are you okay?" he asked.

I didn't know if he was a friend or foe, but he sounded friendly and I needed to trust someone. "I think so."

"Good." He turned to face the thug and squared his shoulders.

"Yeah, fuck off out of it, mate," said the thug. His voice was deep and scratchy. He glared at me. "Surely you can stick up for yourself, love? You don't need your boyfriend for that."

My heart seemed to be beating far too fast. "Do you even know who I am?"

"Uh-huh. I read the flyer. You're just another one trying to line her nest."

"I'm the councillor who's opposing the venture. You've got your facts wrong."

"Are you fucking challenging me?"

"That's enough," said the Viking. "Someone said they'd called the police, so let's hang on and see what they have to say."

"Oh," said the thug sarcastically. "That's a great idea." He shoved the Viking hard enough to knock him sideways then came towards me.

Chapter 3

The Viking kicked the thug in the knee. He cried out then shouted something over his shoulder and a couple of his mates looked over.

"We need to get out of here," said the Viking and grabbed my hand. "We can go out behind the stage. My scout group was based here, so I know all the escape routes."

I checked the balcony and saw Adam leading Maureen away. She waved at me and I waved back, then followed the Viking around the stage to a small door that led into a long narrow room. A banner for Seagrave Scouts was hung on the back wall.

It felt like I'd drunk too much coffee and couldn't quite focus as the Viking led us to a door marked 'fire exit'. As we reached it, someone behind us yelled, "She's through here, come on."

We went through the door into a wide alley hemmed in by high walls on either side. The light of the day had faded and there were a lot of shadows.

"We need to get back to the street," I said. "If the police are coming, I need to speak to them."

"This alley is a dead end, but Welch Road is that way."

We rushed away and I didn't look back when the men came through the door and shouted.

Welch Road was a narrow street of terraced houses and the kerbs were clogged with cars. We'd have to go left to get back to the main entrance of the hall, but a man came towards us from that direction, striding along the white lines with purpose. I didn't know if he was another of the thugs and didn't want to take the chance. The Viking appeared to share that thought.

"The other way," I said.

"Yeah."

We ran to the next junction and I went left, still intending to get back to the hall. My lungs were starting to burn with the exertion and my head ached. The pursuers' footsteps and heavy breathing sounded very loud and drove me on.

The Viking took the lead. I called to go left at the next junction, but he went right and I followed him through a series of random turns. I soon lost my bearings in the back streets and didn't recognise my surroundings.

He stopped and leaned at the waist with his hands on his knees. "We've outrun them, so far."

"They're still coming," I said, trying to catch my breath. "Do you know where we are?"

"I think we're close to the Duncan Jackson estate," he said.

It had been a long time since I was last there, but I knew it backed onto the docks on the southern end of town.

Someone shouted, "There they are!"

The Viking grabbed my hand. We took another couple of turns and then went into a street that wasn't residential but filled with small business units hemmed in by chain-link fences.

"Here we go," he said and pulled me close to a fence. A sign attached to it read 'Davis Motors' and the unit beyond was dark. He took some keys from his pocket. "I work here. Can you get the torch on your phone?"

There were angry shouts from behind us, as if our pursuers had lost the trail.

I pointed the torch at a padlock so he could unlock it. He pushed the gate open enough for me to slip through, then closed it behind him.

We crossed a concrete apron dotted with oil spills to a wide double door. He unlocked the single door next to it and went in. I followed him into a narrow hallway that smelled of engine oil. He closed the door and locked it then leaned on the wall and blew out a breath that lifted his fringe from his forehead.

We stood still, trying to calm our breathing, and I kept my ear close to the door, listening for our pursuers.

"Wow," he said, after what felt like ten minutes. There'd been no untoward sounds from outside. "That was more exciting than I expected it to be."

He laughed nervously and that made me giggle. I clamped my hand over my mouth, even though I knew we were releasing nervous tension. I felt light-headed and leaned against the wall. "I appreciate you helping me."

"No problem." He smiled. "I'm Freddy Medwin, by the way. Seems odd to be introducing myself after that little adventure, doesn't it?"

"Uh-huh. I'm Kim Morgan."

"I heard." We shook hands and his was warm and strong. I was aware of how close we were. The shadows made his cheekbones look sharp and he was watching me. I liked the hot feeling that gave me.

"So, what the hell happened?" he asked. "I thought it was going to be a bit feisty with the protest lady and the developer but… wow! Were those thugs part of the protest group?"

"No. I've been to a lot of the meetings and never seen any of them before."

"They didn't seem to know you either." He touched my forearm, and I could feel his warmth on my skin. "That must have been frightening."

"It was." Even though I was still a bit light-headed, I felt properly alive, as if the fear of the evening had turned into some kind of excitement. His closeness was also making me a little flustered.

"I don't know about you," he said, "but I could do with a drink to calm my nerves."

That sounded like a very good idea. "Is there a pub nearby? We could give it half an hour to make sure they don't find us and then head out."

"I can go one better than that."

He took my hand and we walked to a door marked 'private' at the end of the hallway. It opened onto an office with a narrow desk, a shelving unit crammed with paperwork and catalogues and an old metal filing cabinet. A window looked out over the apron and road and, below it, was a large and well-used leather chair.

"My boss's domain," he said and opened the top drawer of the filing cabinet. He took out a bottle and two plastic cups. "Do you like brandy?"

I preferred wine over spirits but decided beggars couldn't be choosers. "I can live with it."

He poured two generous measures and handed me a cup. Under the light, he looked younger than I'd originally thought, and I realised I might have five years on him. Was that bad? I decided it wasn't. I took a sip and the sweet taste felt warm as I swallowed it. I leaned on the side of the desk. "I really do appreciate this, Freddy."

"Don't worry about it. I saw that bloke heading for you, after you helped the protest lady, and I could hardly ignore it, could I?"

"Maureen!" I exclaimed. How could I have forgotten her? I took my phone out. "I'll text her, to make sure she knows I'm safe."

She'd already texted me. 'Are you okay?' she'd written.

I texted back that I was fine and I hoped she was.

'Yes', she replied a moment or two later. 'The police came but the bullies had gone. Glad you are safe. Speak to you tomorrow.'

"She's okay?" Freddy asked.

"It sounds like it." I sipped more of the brandy and enjoyed the warmth it spread across my chest.

He sat in the leather chair and it squeaked under him. "Well, it's been an interesting evening. My friends aren't going to believe me when I say I helped out a very attractive lady, got chased through Seagrave and then ended up here having a drink."

I heard everything he said but the word 'attractive' seemed neon-rimmed and gave me an excited tingle that I felt all through my body. Perhaps it was a reaction to what had happened. I'd read somewhere that arousal and fear come from the same base emotion, and the attraction between us seemed to be mutual.

"I shouldn't have said that," he said quickly, as if interpreting my silence for concern. "You don't need to worry. I'm not going to attack you."

"Good, because I have a cracking right hook."

He laughed. "We're as dangerous as each other."

I laughed, too, and it felt good, adding to the potent mix of emotions.

Freddy came over to me and held his cup for a toast. "To new beginnings."

"New beginnings." I took another sip. He was standing very close and his proximity warmed me in a different way to the brandy. It had been a while since I'd felt desire like this.

Freddy brushed his fringe off his forehead. He smiled self-consciously and that just stoked the fire. Were we flirting? After what we'd been through, it didn't feel out of place.

"How long do you think we should stay here in case they come back?"

"No idea," he said.

A loud noise from outside made both of us jump. Goosebumps flickered up my arm and I held my breath as Freddy cautiously looked out of the window. If they'd found us and broken in, would we be able to escape?

"It must have been a cat," he said after a few moments. "There's no one out there and the gate's still shut."

My tension drained and suddenly it all felt ridiculous, standing here in a garage office and watching a handsome young man cautiously peer out the window. I giggled and pressed my hand to my mouth to try and stifle it. He glanced over his shoulder and looked at me quizzically and that just made it worse. He laughed in response to me.

"Are you okay?" he asked.

"I'm sorry, I'm not laughing at you. It's everything that's happened." And perhaps about to happen, I thought.

"Well, I think it's sorted now. There's definitely no one out there. Come and look."

I pushed away from the desk and felt a moment of giddiness. I hadn't drunk much but maybe the alcohol had gone straight to my head? Was it that making me giggly? He moved so I could lean on the sill. I shielded my eyes and saw the gate was closed as he'd said.

"I'm pretty sure they didn't see us come in here," he said.

"I think you're right." I could feel his breath on my arm, and if I moved an inch or so to my left, we'd be touching.

"Did you…" He cleared his throat. "Did you want to leave, or…?"

"Or what?" I knew he was feeling this potent cocktail of fear, excitement and brandy, too.

"Did you want another drink?"

"No," I said. "I don't want to move."

"Are you feeling okay?"

"I'm feeling very good, that's why I don't want to move."

Freddy laughed lightly. "I'm feeling very good, too, in that case."

He moved so our hips touched and the contact felt wonderful. He ran a hand lightly up my arm and my skin tingled under his touch. I turned my head slightly as he moved closer. I'd seen the look in his eyes with other men before and responded to it.

"Are you sure you're okay?" he asked quietly.

I was more than okay. I wanted this. "Yes," I said and kissed him.

He responded, his tongue searching into my mouth as he pulled me hard against his chest. His hands slid down my back to cup my buttocks as I ran my fingers through his hair. We moaned in unison and then he pulled me tighter to him.

Chapter 4

The phone alarm woke me.

I opened my eyes slowly and leaned over to tap the screen to snooze. There was a dull ache in my forehead and a not-entirely-unpleasant tenderness in my groin. The events of last night gradually came back to me.

"Oh no," I groaned and rubbed my face carefully.

After Freddy and I finished making out on that slightly uncomfortable leather chair, we sat for a while until we got cold then slowly got dressed. We didn't say a great deal. By then it was close to midnight, and nobody had tried the gate so I was fairly sure we were safe from the thugs and I'd wanted to go home.

We parted company at Regent's Row as he was heading for the old town whereas I was further along Marine Drive, which ran alongside the beach. I assured him I was okay to walk home on my own. He took a little bit of persuading but finally gave in and we stood on the corner by the Golden Nugget arcade regarding one another awkwardly.

"It's been a different evening to what I'd expected," he said.

"Same here."

He brushed his fringe back and the light caught him just right. He was very handsome. I embraced him quickly and he pulled me tight.

"I'll see you," he said.

"Yeah."

We smiled and he walked away. I watched him go a few steps then set off, too.

Now, I sat on the edge of the bed, feeling good and bad in fairly equal measure. I wasn't embarrassed – it was consensual and I didn't make a habit of one-night stands – but it was slightly out of keeping as a lecturer and local councillor.

My mobile rang. "Hello, Maureen, how're you?"

"I'm fine, love, and was ringing to make sure you were. I was so worried about you last night. Where did you go after you'd helped me?"

I told her what happened, right up to Freddy opening the garage for us.

"I don't understand why they chased you, but they kicked off merry hell in the meeting."

"Did you recognise that Costigan bloke?"

"Not at all, and I told the police that, after they insinuated those hooligans were part of our group. Your friend Adam, by the way, is very nice. He kept me company while they asked their questions and I was glad of it."

"Did Glover get hurt? I saw Costigan swing for him."

"No, he was fine. A few of our people helped him out and as soon as the police arrived, the hooligans ran. Glover's personal security man took a few lumps, but he gave plenty out, too. It's all such a mess."

"What did the police say?"

"Not a lot, but they will. The chief constable is apparently a close personal friend of Glover's, as you might expect, so I doubt we'll get a fair hearing." She sighed. "The protest was ridiculed and Glover is making the best of it. My worry is that last night really shot our cause in the foot. All people will see and hear for the next few days is how a brave local property developer stood up to thugs."

I hated to hear the defeat in her voice. "The truth will come out, it always does. And the vote's still to come."

"That might be our final hope," she said. "Anyway, I need to talk tactics with my committee. I'm so pleased you're safe and thank you so much for helping me last night."

"No problem, Maureen. I'll do whatever I can to help, you know that."

"I do. Now, you be careful today and I'll speak to you soon."

* * *

After my shower, I went into the kitchen to make a coffee. It was a bright day and light flooded the room.

I flicked on the radio. Seagrave Sound was playing *Human* by The Killers, which segued into a run of adverts before the news began with the national stories.

"In local news," said the reporter, "there was trouble last night at a meeting for the proposed golf course."

My attention caught, I leaned forward and wrapped both hands around my mug.

"Local property developer Brian Glover was giving a speech in favour of his project when the meeting descended into chaos as members of the protest group stormed the stage. Our reporter, Penny Jones, spoke to Mr Glover last night."

"It was very unpleasant," said Brian Glover. He sounded better on the radio than he did in real life, as if he was enunciating especially hard. "I'd been invited there in what I thought was good faith but maybe I was naïve. After I was given the floor and started to outline the benefits of the plan, several members of the protest group made their presence known."

I shook my head. "They came into the hall," I said to the radio. "You must have seen that."

"Two of them shouted abuse at me, but I'm a grown man and this isn't my first rodeo, so it wasn't like they intimidated me or anything."

Penny Jones finished her report with the suggestion there had been an attempt to keep Glover quiet about the benefits of the golf course before handing back to the newscaster.

"And that's it for *Seagrave Sound News*. The weather for today—"

I stabbed at the off button, angry at Glover's manipulation. He was sharp enough to skew the incident in his favour, even though he must have known Maureen wouldn't allow those thugs to be part of the protest group. In fact, I wouldn't have put it past him to arrange the fracas himself, knowing it would be a real slap in the face to her and the protest.

I took my coffee into the bedroom, dried my hair and got dressed. I was still annoyed with Glover when I walked barefoot into the hall to put on my shoes.

There was a folded sheet of A4 paper on the mat and I regarded it curiously for a moment. My name was printed on the back. It hadn't been there earlier and the postman delivered to a central mailbox in the foyer, so it wasn't from him.

I picked it up and read the message.

> *Who's a naughty girl then? You were seen last night and I'm sure you wouldn't like what you did after the meeting to be made public, would you? Don't tell anyone and we can work something out, so that I don't tell them either.*

Chapter 5

Although my walk to work in the warm sunlight was pleasant, I couldn't get the note out of my head. What could it mean? Who'd seen what I did last night, other than Freddy? And why would *he* write it? He didn't even know where I lived.

The 'we can work something out' phrase troubled me because of the implied threat of blackmail. What had happened, even though it wasn't my wisest decision ever, was hardly the end of the world. I might be a little embarrassed for a while, because who wanted their sex life made public, but what did they hope to gain? Would a further note instruct me to put a sum of money in a secure place or risk seeing my face on the front page of the *Seagrave Telegraph*?

* * *

Seagrave College is split over two campuses, one focussing on humanities and the other on design and technology. I lecture in English language at the Town Campus, which isn't as central as the name would suggest while the other campus is a few streets over, closer to the docks.

I turned into Norfolk Road, where the Town Campus is located, and waited at the kerb as a battered car went past, driven by a teenager who didn't look old enough to drive. He was searching for a parking spot and clearly hadn't yet realised they were like gold dust. If you wanted to park anywhere near campus, you either had to buy a pass or get there before dawn.

The college began life as a comprehensive school in the sixties and its various growth spurts over the decades had given the place a disjointed appearance, with differing architectural styles and a variety of corridors and walkways to link the buildings. The car park spread across the front and around the sides, and the college was shielded from the houses behind and to the side by a playing field hemmed in by trees.

I went into the main building and nobody was behind the reception desk so I walked upstairs to the administration office. A few of the staff were at their desks and we greeted one another as I walked along.

There were four large envelopes in my pigeonhole. Maria, who sat at the nearest desk, smiled when she saw me.

"Morning, Kim."

"Morning." I checked the envelopes. Three were addressed to me but the fourth was for a colleague called Kim Martin, based at the other campus.

"Have you bumped into George yet?" Maria asked.

"No, why? Is he after me?"

George Royston was the vice-principal and his office was on this floor.

She gave a delicate shrug. "He asked if you were in today and then went on his way. But he had that look on his face, you know? The one that says something is playing on his mind." She raised her eyebrows. "Maybe he's got some news for you?"

The current head of humanities was leaving at the end of the year and I'd put in for the head of department position. It was an increase in responsibility and pay and I thought I could make a good job of it. "Maybe," I said.

"Who's got news for who?" asked Adam Wright.

A handsome man in his mid-forties, he was big and in good shape and still played rugby for the Lecturers 15. His thick brown hair was only just starting to grey at the temples and it really suited him. His pale-blue short-sleeved Oxford shirt made his arms look impressive and a messenger bag was slung over one shoulder.

"Maria said Gorgeous George was looking for me."

"Oh, yes?" Adam taught geography and was also in the running for the position. We'd talked about it at the time and it was a source of friendly rivalry between us now, although I definitely wanted the role. "Did he mention me?" he asked Maria.

"Not to me," she said and turned her attention back to her computer.

Adam checked his pigeonhole, and I could smell his aftershave. "Do you think he's come to a decision?"

"No idea, I haven't seen him yet."

When my marriage hit its final death throes, Adam was a real rock. He'd just been through a bruising divorce of his own and seemed to know just the right time to suggest cooking me dinner, or to go for a drink, or to the cinema or take in a show. We were just friends then, despite what our faculty colleagues thought, but a relationship quickly blossomed that was wonderful while it lasted. Unfortunately, the fit wasn't quite right for me in ways I could never properly explain, so I'd ended it earlier this year. Thankfully, we were grown up enough to keep hold of our friendship, which only seemed to get stronger. I still found him handsome, but that door was closed for me and despite the fact he was seeing someone else, I got the sense that if I changed my mind, he'd be more than willing to pick things up from where they had ended.

"I need to drop this at the other campus first," I said and held up the rogue envelope as though to prove my point. "Did you fancy walking with me?" It was Monday morning and both of us had a free first period.

"I'd like that."

We made our way outside.

"I wanted to thank you for looking after Maureen last night."

"I wish I could have done more. When I saw that bloke heading for you, my instinct was to get in his way but that would have meant leaving Maureen alone."

"You did the right thing."

"So, what happened? I saw you run off with that young man." He said it mockingly and when I glanced at him, he smiled. "What? I saw how you looked at him. I mean, I can appreciate a handsome-looking lad."

I felt a quick flush of embarrassment. "He was hardly a lad."

"He wasn't as old as me."

"Not many things are."

"Oi." He tried to sound offended. "I'm fifteen years older than you. That hardly makes me ancient."

"It makes you closer to your fifties than I am to my forties."

"Ouch. You really know how to kick a man in the nuts, don't you?"

"Yeah, yeah."

He laughed. "So, what did you and the handsome young man do?"

My mind flashed back to the note. "What do you mean?"

"What happened with those men chasing you?"

I don't know if it was because of the note or some kind of loyalty to him and our past, but I didn't want to tell him what had happened. "We ran until we couldn't hear them, then headed for home. Did any of the ones in the hall say anything to you?"

"No, they ran off when the police arrived."

"So I heard."

We crossed the road and walked towards the other campus.

"It was all a bit odd, wasn't it?" he asked. "Maureen said she didn't know any of them, but who'd gain from having ringers go in and start a fight?"

"Well, Brian Glover was on the radio this morning making the most of the whole thing."

"He could fall into a pile of shit and come out smelling of roses, Kim, you know that." He frowned, as if he'd taken himself by surprise. "Actually, thinking about it, this is a win-win situation for him. If any of your council colleagues were sitting on the fence about the vote, thugs from the protest group trying to beat up Glover aren't going to endear them to the cause."

"Do you think he set it all up?"

"I didn't say that, but if anyone was willing to discredit their opposition to make a lot of money, I wouldn't bet against Brian Glover."

Put like that, it sounded painfully believable, but would Glover risk it? With social media it was hard enough for one person to keep a secret, and if the police got hold of Costigan and charged him, he'd surely spill the beans and lay out the whole plan.

"I never took you for a conspiracy theorist," I said.

He laughed. "I'm not, but this doesn't make sense and I don't like that."

We reached the other campus. A group of students came around the main building, heavy bags slung over their shoulders as they talked and laughed with one another. I was about to look away when one of them caught my eye and it took me a moment to understand who I was looking at.

The realisation struck me like a slap, and I felt sick and unbearably hot.

It might not have been bad that I'd had a one-night stand, but it was suddenly much worse than that.

I'd had a one-night stand with a student.

Chapter 6

"What's up, Kim? You look like you've seen a ghost."

"I'm fine," I said, but there was a hollow sensation in my stomach, and it felt like I'd be sick if I moved too quickly.

A lecturer being involved with a student might not be as career-ending as it once was, but I'd crossed a massive line and gone completely against my principles. Even if I could prove I'd had no idea Freddy was a student, because we were on different campuses, did that make it any better?

Other than my ethical concern, the situation was also strictly against college rules and that had been drummed into me as soon as I started here. There'd been some kind of scandal in the past and it was an absolute no-no for a lecturer and student to see each another romantically. Even a close friendship was frowned upon, but I'd gone way past that. And, according to the rules, I should report it immediately. But if I did that, I might barely hang onto my job as it was, let alone be in line for head of department.

A horrifying thought struck me. I'd guessed he was younger but what if the age gap was even greater than I'd thought and he was a first year? Had I just corrupted an eighteen-year-old?

"You really don't look it," Adam said.

"I am," I insisted and hoped the lie wasn't evident in my voice.

The group went through doors marked 'students only' and Freddy didn't look my way. The administration block was off to the left and I walked towards it.

"You were fine and chatty, then you just stopped," Adam said with concern.

"I was thinking about something else," I said, trying to close down this line of questioning. "You know how it is."

I pushed through the doors and crossed the foyer to the reception desk. An older woman I knew enough to say hello to was sitting behind it.

"Can I give you this?" I asked and handed her the envelope. "It got delivered to the wrong Kim."

"Oh, okay, I'll put it in his pigeonhole."

"Thanks."

Adam had waited at the door for me and now opened it so we could go through. "How about I buy you a coffee on our campus?"

"I have something I need to do first," I said. I'd just had a thought and needed to check something. "I'll see you later."

* * *

I went back into the administration office on the Town Campus and made my way directly to Pam Northcott's desk. She was the bursar and close to retirement age but didn't look any older now than she did on the first day I met her. She'd taken me under her wing then and still treated me wonderfully and I liked her a lot.

She greeted me with a warm smile. "Hello there, Kim. How're you feeling? I understand you had a bit of an evening of it last night."

I knew she had to mean the meeting, but it still made me pause for a moment. "Sort of."

"Well, I think it's bloody disgusting, if you'll excuse my language. I said to my Ron this morning, if they want a bloody golf course, why does Brian Glover have to build it there?" She shook her head. "I wish I'd seen that bloke clobber him."

"I don't think he got clobbered, Pam."

"He said he did on the radio this morning."

"I think he was doing it for effect."

"Really?" She seemed genuinely surprised. "So that bloody rotter lied on the radio?"

"Yes, and the bloke who went for him wasn't part of the protest group either."

"Brian Glover is a scoundrel; he always has been. And he'll get away with it, you mark my words." She looked disappointed. "Anyway, what can I do for you this morning?"

"I need to find out something about a student and wondered if you could help me."

"I'll try, but it'll depend on what it is, with the GDPR rules and such."

"I don't want to delve too far, just grab a couple of details."

Pam pulled her keyboard a little closer and her fingers hovered over it. "Which student were you after?"

"Freddy Medwin."

She typed his name then studied the screen. "What did you want to know?"

I had so many questions but needed to be careful how I asked them. The last thing I wanted to do now was drop some kind of hint that I'd broken the rules. "Can you tell me what he's studying?"

"Mechanics and Engineering, on the other campus."

I felt a little bloom of relief. While I wasn't out of the woods yet, I could argue I've never seen him before and, also, that he'd never seen me either. It wasn't unknown for students to pursue their tutors, even if I didn't get that impression from him. "How far through his course is he?"

"It's his final year. He was on placement last year, to a mechanic on the other side of Seagrave. According to the notes it went well and he's still working there to top up his loans."

Final year would mean he was at least twenty-one, so at least I hadn't corrupted a teenager. "He looks older," I said.

"I don't know him," she said and scanned the screen. "He's listed as a mature student, so perhaps he took a gap year."

I'd feel a lot better if that were the case, but I knew she probably wouldn't be able to tell me even if I asked, because of the rules.

"Thanks, Pam. You've been a great help, as always."

"Always here for you, Kim, you know that." Her phone rang and she reached for the receiver. "You have a good day."

"You too."

George came into the office. "Miss Morgan," he said. "Just the person I wanted to see."

"Maria said you looking for me earlier. I was just on my way to see you."

His expression suggested he didn't quite believe me. "That's excellent timing, then. Shall we go into my office?" He made a sweeping gesture for me to go first.

"Lead the way," I said.

He gave a little frustrated shake of his head before walking away and I followed him along the corridor to his office.

"Close the door," he said, and I did.

His office was big but spartan, with a large desk in front of a picture window that looked out over the playing field. A couple of certificates and a framed degree hung on the walls.

George moved behind his desk, put his hands in the small of his back and stretched. He was tall and thin enough that his head looked slightly too big for his body, an illusion not helped by his predilection for tight, well-cut suits.

"How are you this morning?" he asked.

"I'm fine. How're you?"

He seemed surprised I'd asked. "I'm doing well, thank you. Now I understand you were involved in some trouble last night?"

I started to correct him, but he held up his hand as if he didn't need me to explain. "Now while I fully appreciate my faculty members being involved in the community, I am a little concerned about your association with the protest group."

"I'm trying to help the community."

"A brawl hardly helps a community."

"It wasn't really a brawl," I said.

"Then what would you call it?"

"Some random thugs came into the meeting and were violent."

"Against the very person the protest group has an issue with."

"That doesn't mean they were with us and I'm sure you know that, George. Glover is playing to that narrative because he's very good at getting his own way with things."

"You may well be right, but people pay attention to him, and bad news often has ramifications." He held up his hand as if to silence me pre-emptively and I bit my lip in frustration. "There's no doubt in my mind you're telling the truth, Kim. In all the time I've known you, you've never been less than extremely straightforward and honest, showing the utmost respect for this institution. I don't believe you would knowingly bring the college into disrepute."

The pretty words couldn't hide the inference. "I'm not."

"As I said, but I'm torn with this development because, frankly, it doesn't look good. You know we're due an Ofsted inspection and I can't have one of my senior members of staff, who is in contention for a head of department role, being seen to condone violent activities."

"I don't condone the activities and neither does the rest of the group."

"That's as may be, but I need to consider the optics if the Ofsted inspector asks how we're perceived in the community. What do I tell him or her about what happened last night and how do we know it won't happen again?"

"Because the vote's on Thursday."

He allowed himself a tight smile. "Do you really think that if the protest group loses the vote, they'll accept it quietly and walk away?" His smug smile showed he knew I couldn't answer that. "All I'm trying to say is you should rein things in a bit for a while."

"Are you telling me I can't continue with the protest group?"

"Of course not, because, God knows, I don't want Brian Glover to desecrate that wonderful marshland any more than the next man. But I have to think of the college and my position and so I ask you, until the Ofsted inspection is over, to consider your actions."

"By not getting involved in violent protest?"

"Indeed."

It wouldn't make any difference to press my case and there was the worry that he'd ask how I got away, because I certainly wasn't discussing that with him. "You're right, George."

"Thank you, Kim. I knew you'd see it my way."

I knew it seemed like capitulation, but I had to smile it off. "If that's all, I'd better go. I have a class."

He dismissed me with a wave in the general direction of the door. "Thank you for being understanding."

* * *

I turned the situation over as I walked to the English block, trying to figure out the connections between this morning's revelations. I took the note out of my bag and even holding it made me feel nauseous.

Could it really have been from Freddy? If it wasn't, what did that mean? My stomach churned. Had someone else seen me leave with him and put two and two together?

And what if they knew he was a student?

Chapter 7

Since it was the second Monday of the month, I walked into town at lunchtime and felt like everyone was looking at me, as if my secret was like a big neon sign.

I was meeting Caitlin Alexander, a fellow councillor who'd drafted me into her 'Clean Up The Beach' project, at Pip's Place, a little cafe on Ware Street that served the best lemon drizzle cake I'd ever eaten. Pip had a rescue Jack Russell called Snoopy that would sniff for treats before settling at Caitlin's feet and snooze as we talked. I wasn't sure if Pip and Caitlin were related or if Caitlin had lent money to get the place up and running, but there was a strong link between the women.

I pushed open the door and the familiar homely smells of good coffee and baking assailed me. Pip was behind the counter making a frothy coffee. "The usual table," she said.

Caitlin was already here, sitting with her back to me as she looked through the window onto Ware Street. A slim briefcase was against the chair leg and Snoopy was lying on her right foot. She stroked behind his ear absently.

"Hi," I said and pulled out a chair to sit down. "Sorry I'm late."

"That's okay." Caitlin was in her late fifties and took good care of herself. Her skin glowed, her cheekbones could have cut glass, and she'd gone grey gracefully, sporting a shaggy cut that suited her perfectly.

Pip put a tray with two steaming mugs and two plates, one with lemon drizzle cake and the other with coffee cake, on the table. "Enjoy, ladies."

We both thanked her and, after she'd gone, Caitlin took a document wallet from her case and laid it on the table.

"Before we start, I heard last night was a bit of a fiasco." She raised her eyebrows in an 'I told you so' expression. We were on distinctly different sides of the argument and hadn't been able to find any common ground on it at all.

"You didn't go in the end, then?"

"No, and, to be honest, after listening to the news this morning I'm glad I didn't."

"Brian was making a mountain out of a molehill in the report I heard." I chose my words carefully since she'd told me he was a close personal friend of hers.

"I agree he has a flair for the dramatic, but if he says he was assaulted then I believe him." She shook her head with disappointment. "It's awful when a group can't control their people."

"Those thugs weren't part of the group."

She gave a sour bark of a laugh. "Are you suggesting some random group of hooligans saw the meeting and decided to poke their noses in?" Sarcasm dripped from her words.

"No, I'm saying he's made more of it than he needed to."

"Of course he has, he's been handed a golden ticket with the vote on Thursday. All he has to do is keep public sympathy on his side and the proposal passes."

"Let's hope not."

She arched her left eyebrow. "Oh, come on, Kim. Even you can see this is a lost cause now."

"I really hope that's not right."

"You know I respect you, Kim, both as a person and for what you bring to the council. But I cannot fathom your disagreement with a proposal that could bring so much good to the town. At the end of the day, Brian wants the best for the area. Like the rest of us do."

"He's also a businessman who wants to make money for himself and his investors."

"And what's wrong with that, if Seagrave benefits?"

We'd had this debate a few times and it was an endless loop. She was my senior in the council and in line to be the next mayor, so I had to choose the right time to argue the point. I wasn't in the mood today. "We'll see what happens at the vote."

"We will." She took a bite of her cake and gave me a quick smile that was as close to a peacekeeping one as she was likely to give. "Pip does make a lovely coffee cake."

I smiled. "It's not as nice as her lemon drizzle cake."

"Has anyone ever told you that you could start a fight in an empty room?"

"The last person, I think, was you."

She grinned at me. "I taught you well."

I hadn't intended to serve on the council and my first brush with politics was when Seagrave Library was threatened with closure. I'd volunteered to help and, because of my connection to the college, was elected to be spokesperson at the public meetings. Caitlin was opposed to the closure, and we'd bonded quickly. A seat became available after the library was saved and she'd suggested I put myself forward. After I'd won, she became something of a mentor. When she'd found out we were both divorcees, she'd taken me for a meal on Valentine's Day and we'd had a wonderful evening before going back to her lovely house on a very nice street with a wide driveway and a couple of trees in the back garden. A victory of her divorce, she'd told me with a little glint in her eye. I'd told her she'd come out of hers with more than I had, even relatively speaking, and she'd replied that I should have used her solicitor.

"So, to the business at hand," she said. "How's progress been?"

The 'Clean Up The Beach' project came about when one of her constituents had complained their child developed an infection from touching dog waste on the beach. It was a considerable problem, especially during the summer season, and we were aiming to 'educate the owner and eradicate the mess'. I thought we needed a stronger name – I'd laughingly suggested "keep your shit off the sand" when we were brainstorming ideas – but she'd said we couldn't offend anyone.

I took my pad from my bag and found the notes I'd made late last week. "My friend Sarah is head at the infants' school and she's going to arrange for the kids to design a poster."

"Marvellous. If you pass me her name, then I'll write to her officially and set the ball rolling on that. Did you think of a good prize to offer?"

"You know the bloke who runs the fair, don't you?" I said. Caitlin ran the equestrian centre on the Radnor Road and there weren't many businesspeople she didn't know in Seagrave. "I thought we could offer a day pass to the winner and their family."

"That's a great idea," she said and tapped her teeth with her pen. "In fact, I could probably wrangle more out of him."

"That would be great."

With the mood lightened, we ran through the rest of the business quickly and I ate my lovely cake.

"And how's work?" Caitlin asked as she drained her coffee. "Did your principal mention anything about the new role?" I'd told her when I first heard of the vacancy, and she'd encouraged me to put my name forward.

"No. But I don't think he's happy with me being involved last night."

"That makes two of us. Let's hope his judgement is based purely on your ability, Kim, because you deserve that role. You're very good at your job."

"Thank you."

Caitlin leaned towards me. "Let me know if you don't get it and I'll have some words to say to him." She smiled but it looked cold.

Chapter 8

I had two classes in the afternoon and one of them involved talking about John Proctor from *The Crucible* and the importance of his name. I tried not to think about how I'd potentially managed to compromise my own name, but it was there all the time, like a deep pulse I couldn't ignore.

As I didn't have any student appointments or faculty meetings, I left campus on time and cut a zigzag route down to Marine Drive. I've lived on the coast for most of my life and have found there aren't many things more soothing than watching the waves for a while.

I walked out onto the Empire Pier and leaned on the rail. A light breeze blew my hair around my face as I breathed in deeply the scent of seawater that filled the air. The horizon seemed endless, with only a few clouds hovering above it, and there was the faintest silhouette of a large ship sailing by.

The tide was coming in and water slapped at the support legs. I leaned over and saw a couple of kids with buckets digging in the sand as if they were trying to catch something. One glanced up and saw me. I smiled but his face darkened into a frown, and he said something to his friend before they both disappeared out of sight.

Maybe they'd heard about last night, too.

I stood there for about fifteen minutes until I felt sufficiently relaxed then walked back to the street and turned towards town. With the season over, most of the tourists had left and it was a pleasant walk. The arcades were still going and the machines on the aprons made plenty of noise to entice in the schoolkids walking by. On the beach side of Marine Drive, the seasonal stalls which sold homemade and craft items to the holidaymakers were boarded up and wouldn't re-open until Christmas and New Year.

A man in a hi-vis jacket was sweeping a small pile of litter with a wide broom. I smiled when he glanced at me but he scowled and went back to his work. Like the kids under the pier, there was no reason for him to return my friendly gesture, but it felt a little off that he hadn't.

It was almost like I was being judged, but I knew that was paranoia. They didn't know me or what I'd done with Freddy Medwin and then, just like that, him and the line I'd crossed were back in the forefront of my mind.

My natural default is to worry and I could feel the stress beginning to take root. The start of a headache gnawed at my temples and I questioned myself as to the best way of dealing with the situation. In an ideal world, I would report it, but that was never going to end well. Would George be likely to believe I'd made a mistake and, even if he did, surely his hands were tied? I'd broken a rule and if the college wanted to invoke safeguarding measures, I might have broken the law, too. Was it fair that Freddy's life and mine, not to mention my career, would be damaged by a casual one-night stand that I was under the impression was simply a consensual act between two adults? Even in the best-case scenario of George believing I'd made a terrible mistake, with Ofsted breathing down his neck he would have to suspend me. I could forget the head of department role, even if I didn't have to leave the college, and the stigma of what I'd done would follow me like a bad smell forever.

A male friend of mine from training college had been caught dallying. He was amiable enough but had more brains than street smarts and he'd been seeing a female student who, as it turned out, was only about three years younger than him. He hadn't realised she was a student when they'd first met but, crucially, he didn't stop once he discovered. And he didn't report it either. He was drummed out of his career in a painful blaze of publicity and the last I heard, he was working with computers in the City. I was sympathetic to his situation at first, until I realised he knew the truth and then I was angry with him. Professional boundaries and rules weren't there to be ignored or taken lightly and I knew I'd be judged the same way.

On the other hand, to the best of my knowledge, he'd never been blackmailed.

And that just brought me back to the beginning. Why would Freddy blackmail me? I wasn't rich, I couldn't help him with his grades, so what did he expect me to do?

None of it made any sense.

A horn blared and, startled, I looked up to see I was about to walk into the path of a delivery van. The driver gave me the finger and mouthed something I couldn't hear before speeding away with a squeal of tyres.

I was a couple of streets from where Pops, my granddad, lived and decided to call in and see him.

His flat was on the top floor of a converted townhouse with a commanding sea view and a suntrap balcony. He'd been a photographer for the *Seagrave Telegraph* during its heyday in the sixties and seventies and made two or three very smart property-market moves, setting himself up for a nice retirement. We'd always got on well and, after my parents moved to Wales for "a change of scene", we saw a lot of one another.

I pressed his buzzer and he answered after a few moments. "Hello?"

"Pops? It's me. Can I come up?"

"Of course you can!" The affection in his voice, even with the crackle of the intercom, was evident and warming. "I'll stick the kettle on!"

The buzzer sounded and I pushed the door open onto a wide hallway with chequered marble floor tiles. I went up the stairs quickly to his landing and saw someone coming towards me who looked vaguely familiar. He was about my age, with sandy-coloured hair and his T-shirt had a retro Kodak logo on it.

"Hi," he said. "You off to see your granddad?"

"How did you know that?"

"Because I..." He shook his head. "Sorry, I must sound like a stalker but I'm really not. My name's Ryan Taylor. Your granddad helps me out sometimes with..."

"Your photography," I finished for him. "He's mentioned you in the past. It's nice to finally meet you."

"Likewise." He smiled and there was a bashful element to it. "I was showing him my pictures from last night as it happens and got a few of you. It was a bit of a night, wasn't it?"

"It was," I said and realised that's why he'd looked so familiar.

"When that man went for the stage, I came down to try and help but got caught up in the fight in the aisle."

"I was lucky and managed to get out the back way." He didn't need to know any more. "None of it should have happened. Those thugs weren't anything to do with the protest."

"Glad to hear it. I've supported it for a while and the events left a sour taste in the mouth." He took out his wallet and handed me a card. "Actually, if you ever need any pictures doing for whatever reason, let me know and I'll be happy to get involved."

"Thanks." The card had his name, a mobile number and website URL. "We might need to take you up on it, assuming last night's mess hasn't destroyed the group's credibility."

"I doubt it will. Me and your granddad were talking about it just now. I'm putting together a proposal for the paper so hopefully we can get some of the news across."

"Do you work for the *Seagrave Telegraph*?"

"I used to, but I freelance now. When the paper got bought out by the *Norwich Chronicle*, it essentially became an ad sheet with recycled articles from other titles in the group. It's not like it was when your granddad ruled the photo pages." He ran a hand through his thick hair. "Speaking of whom, I'd better let you get on. It was good to meet you."

"And you."

He went down the stairs and I knocked on Pops' door.

"Come in, treacle," he called, and I went in. "Go through and I'll be there in a minute."

I went into the sun-drenched lounge, which was compact and comfortable with a three-piece suite, an overflowing bookcase, a framed picture of Seagrave beach he'd taken himself and a family display of photographs in one corner. There were my parents, in various stages – my dad as a kid, him and my mum when they started going out, their wedding day – before a whole load with me in. My beloved and much-missed grandmother was also there. I loved looking at the display but sometimes, if my mood was a bit low, it was a little too poignant to enjoy.

I sat on the armchair nearest the opened patio doors and looked out at the view, which made the town look good whatever the weather. He had a couple of chairs and a bistro table out there and his camera was mounted on a tripod looking towards the pier.

Pops came in carrying two mugs and a pair of socks held between his fingers. He was wearing a pair of chino shorts and a nice white Oxford shirt with short sleeves.

"Thanks," I said, as he handed me a mug. "You're looking very smart, as always. Are you going out somewhere?"

He sat on the sofa across from me and sipped his drink. "Yes, I'm taking the widow Johnson out for a meal."

"Somewhere posh?"

My granddad was seventy-nine and kept himself in great shape, mentally and physically. He became a widower when I was in my teens and had mourned my grandmother terribly for a long time and still does, but was coping better these days. A couple of years ago he'd renewed a friendship with an old family friend, Christine Johnson, when her husband passed away. That friendship was now becoming something deeper, and I was enjoying watching it develop.

"I don't know about posh," he said with a grin. "I took her for a ride on Betty yesterday up the coast to Sheringham. It was a lovely day and I think she enjoyed herself and, on the way back, she spotted a country pub that reckons it has the best food for miles around."

Betty was a 1963 Lambretta scooter he'd bought as a teenager and, according to family legend, used to take his then-girlfriend to Brighton where they'd got caught up in some of the fights between mods and rockers. My dad had had his doubts about whether that had actually happened, but Pops had married his girlfriend, who became my grandmother, and had christened the bike after her. I'm convinced he's maintained it so well over the years because he associated it so much with his lost love.

"So, what's new with you?" he asked and leaned forward to pull on a sock. "Ryan was just showing me his pictures of last night."

"He said. We met on the landing."

"I heard Glover on the radio, but that little twerp knew how to twist things his way even when he was doing odd jobs for Hugh Cowley."

I told him the basics of what had happened, up to where Freddy had helped me get out of the hall.

"Maureen must have been angry."

"She wasn't happy. Thankfully, Adam was there and helped to get her out of the way of trouble."

"Ah, Adam was there, was he?" Pops had never been quite convinced about Adam. They'd met just after we'd started going out and both men had tried, but didn't really connect. Pops reckons it was because Adam was into rugby, and he preferred cricket, but I think it was really down to Pops not being happy with the age gap. "So, what do you think'll be the outcome?"

I thought back to Caitlin's comment that Glover had been handed a golden ticket. "I suppose it's hard to tell until the vote happens."

"So long as everyone plays fair," he said and pulled on his second sock. "Did Ryan tell you about his proposal? I'll speak to Maureen and see if I can help her, too." Pops had been documenting a changing Seagrave in photographs since the mid-seventies and I found his project fascinating

"Have you taken some photographs today?" I asked, gesturing towards the camera on the patio.

"I've been trying out some more of my blurred landscapes," he said. Pops didn't lay down his cameras when he retired from the *Telegraph*. His current project involved taking views of the town on a delayed exposure, so the landscape and buildings were in sharp focus and offset by the blur of motion from pedestrians, vehicles or – in perhaps my favourite of the series, which he took near the pier – a gull diving for food. "Ryan lent me his GoPro and said it had all manner of tricks, but you know me, I prefer my analogue technology."

Pops did his own darkroom work and I'd once made the mistake of saying how much easier it would be to do things digitally. He wasn't having any of it and we never had that discussion again. If he liked the analogue process, then who was I to try and change his mind?

"So, you're experimenting, then?"

"Oh," he said with a wave of his hand, "I only did it to shut him up. He showed me all the bells and whistles and I just stopped taking it in and said that I would line the damned thing up and focus and then he would do all the stuff with his laptop."

41

"Do you expect to get anything better with the GoPro than you would with your Leica?"

"No." He shrugged. "I'm not sure what I'll get. Ryan wanted to extend the exposure time to levels where all I'd get is a wash of light, but I talked him out of it. We've set it to take a shot every minute and he reckons we can then blend the images in Photoshop." He smiled. "I'm obviously not touching that with a bargepole. Do you know what he called me?"

I smiled and shook my head.

"A Luddite." His exasperation made me laugh and that made him laugh in turn. "A bloody Luddite! I was inventing camera tricks before he was even born. A Luddite? I flipping ask you."

"Do you use any technology you didn't have to hand in the 1970s?"

"Don't you get cheeky on me now, young lady," he said and tried to hide his grin but couldn't.

"So what time are you due to pick up the widow Johnson?"

He checked his watch and gave me a rueful smile. "Whenever you decide to leave, I won't be far behind."

"I can take a hint."

Chapter 9

I usually made it a point to avoid drinking on a school night, but decided alcohol might make the evening a little more bearable, so I picked up a bottle of wine from the off-licence. I only bought a half, not trusting myself to leave anything for another day. Once home, I kicked off my shoes, dropped my bag by the door and went into my bedroom to get changed out of my work clothes. Wearing a fresh T-shirt and pair of shorts, I walked barefoot into the kitchen, poured myself a generous glass of white and went into the lounge. I opened the French windows and looked out at Seagrave. The Hippodrome theatre was a couple of streets over and a show was being prepared, so an army of people moved items from the back of a big truck. The noise of them competed with the cawing of seagulls, carried on a light breeze that played with the curtains.

I went to my desk, opened my laptop and logged into my email.

There seemed to be more than usual. Two were from Seagrave Sound, asking if I'd consent to an on-air interview. I declined them both. The *Seagrave Telegraph* had sent some questions for an in-print interview, but I declined that, too. A dozen or more were from people I didn't know who'd probably picked up my email from the council page; they were roughly split between support and animosity.

One was from the leader of the council who wanted to remind me of my responsibilities and that I needed to separate constituents' wishes from my 'campaigning', as he called it.

"Stupid bastard," I muttered at the screen as I deleted the message.

There was a run of emails from fellow councillors on the planning committee, with the first from Caitlin, who chaired it.

> *Dear fellow committee members,*
> *I wasn't present but have heard first-hand details of the terrible display at the Methodist Hall last night where a few protest group members verbally bullied Brian Glover and physically attacked his driver. I knew Maureen Northcott didn't run a tight ship, but this is beyond the pale. Do we really want prominent, highly regarded and influential Seagrave residents to be attacked – yes, I will say attacked – when they are simply stating their point at an open public meeting?*

Bearing in mind what happened — and what will, no doubt, be reported by various sections of the media — I don't see how anyone in good conscience can vote against the golf course proposal.

Her tone annoyed me, by seeming to suggest that if we didn't agree with her then we were voting for anarchy. That was so wrong as to be insulting. I clicked reply and wrote 'Dear Caitlin' before stopping. Whether she was right or not, responding angrily wouldn't be a good idea on so many levels. I needed to cool off for a moment.

The next email was from one of her friends who always toed the party line and did so again. My annoyance levels rose. Three neutral members of the committee disagreed with the actions of the thugs but weren't sure they were associated with the protest group. I debated emailing them to thank them but didn't do that either. I had to consider the optics, as George would have said. The last email was from someone who'd been sitting on the fence before last night's display had made her decision and she'd now be voting for the proposal.

I leaned back in my chair, rubbed my face then rang Maureen.

"Hello, love." She sounded down.

"How are you?"

"Oh, bearing up. I've been interviewed by someone from Seagrave Sound, even though I really wasn't sure I wanted to and I don't think it'll do much good." She sighed. "Brian has really turned the situation to his advantage."

"So, what's next?"

"I'd like to have a chat with you before the vote, if you are up for that. I've had a shit day – pardon my expression – and I'm sure yours hasn't been a bed of roses either."

If only you knew, I thought. "You could say that. I'd be happy to chat with you, though. What did you have in mind?"

"I feel like getting out of the house and going for a drink. Would you be interested?"

It felt like a wonderful idea to me. "Tell me the place, Maureen, and I'll meet you there."

* * *

The Traveller's Rest was one of those chain pubs where the menu and drinks choice was the same wherever you went in the country. It was also popular. I got there a little before seven and Maureen waved at me from a two-person table she'd secured by the back wall. A bottle of white wine and two glasses were in front of her.

"I hope you don't mind but I ordered."

"Not a problem," I said as I sat down. "I'm a big fan of white wine."

"I remembered you saying." She poured us both a generous glass then raised hers. "To us."

"To us."

We ordered food and talked about everything but the meeting and then ate in companionable silence. The bottle didn't last long and when she went to order a second, I suggested we buy by the glass instead.

"Ah, of course, it's a school day tomorrow, isn't it?" She smiled at me. "You tend to forget these things, love, once you retire."

"Don't worry. I'll get the first round in."

I grabbed my bag and made my way to the bar and got served quickly. I picked up the two glasses and was about to turn away when a hand touched my elbow.

"I'm sorry," I said, assuming I was about to knock someone. I turned to see a woman in her late forties glaring at me. She wasn't close enough for me to catch her, even if I'd taken a step to the left. "Oh, I thought you were trying to stop me from knocking you."

She had very red lips. "No, Councillor Morgan, I wasn't."

I groaned inwardly and put the glasses down. In my experience, when someone addresses me like that, it means I'm not likely to get away too quickly. "I see. So, what can I do for you?"

She chuckled sourly. "I think you've done enough, haven't you? I was there last night, you know. I saw what a farce that all descended into. I thought you and that Maureen woman would be spending your time trying to undo the smear you've put on Seagrave rather than sit here and drink it up."

"Smear?" Was she really having a go at me in the middle of a crowded pub? "I'm not sure I understand what you mean. How exactly did I smear Seagrave?"

She leaned in slightly. "By not controlling that meeting where a much-respected member of our community was almost attacked. Whether you were there as a councillor or protestor, you have a duty to our town."

The woman was clearly angry but also, it seemed, a little tipsy, too, and I decided the best thing to do was try and defuse the situation as quickly as possible, rather than debate it. "I'm sorry you think that way, Mrs…" I let my sentence fade, but she didn't offer her name. "It wasn't my intention to belittle the town, or Mr Glover. You need to believe that I always work for the betterment of Seagrave."

"Yeah," she said, clearly not believing a word I'd said. "So will you change your vote then?"

I took a breath. "No," I said, simply and clearly.

"No?"

"No. I will be voting against the golf course."

"I feel sorry for you," the woman said. "It's almost like you're damaged somehow."

I took a breath, determined not to rise to her provocation, and then a man I didn't recognise intervened. "There you are, Leigh," he said and put a hand on her shoulder. "I wondered where you'd got to. Our food's arrived."

The anger in her expression faded as she turned to him. "I was just talking to the councillor here."

"Oh, were you?" He looked at me with an unreadable expression. "I'm sorry to interrupt, miss, but I need to get my friend back now. Our dinner's been served."

"That's not a problem," I said with relief then looked at Leigh. Always be polite, I thought, even if you know it's going to piss the other person off. "Thank you for offering your views, Leigh. I'll take them under advisement."

She looked as though she wanted me to drop off the face of the planet but didn't say anything and let the man lead her away. He glanced over his shoulder. "My apologies for interrupting you," he said.

"You're fine." I raised a glass to him, then went back to our table. As someone said to me when I first joined, being a councillor is only marred by some of the people you represent.

* * *

The evening was warm and calm as I walked Maureen home and twilight painted the sky in a variety of reds and purples.

"I'm sorry we're having to walk so slowly."

I linked arms with her. "I don't mind a steady walk."

"Nice choice of word," she said and smiled at me. "I can tell you're an English lecturer."

"Caught out," I said.

"Who was the lady you were talking to at the bar?"

"A constituent," I said. "She wanted to discuss the golf course."

"I'm sure," she said, with an amused tone. "I could see your face and you looked like you were about ready to spit feathers."

"She did have some, uh, forthright views."

"Some people always do," she said then changed the subject and we talked about pleasant things until we got to her cottage. I waited by the gate until she'd opened her front door.

"I'll see you soon, Kim. And thank you for this. I needed to get out and away from things for a bit."

"Me, too," I said.

She locked the door, and I walked home. By the time I got back to my flat it was dark, and I finished the bottle of wine sitting by the French windows and watching the lights in Seagrave.

Chapter 10

Something startled me awake.

I sat up too quickly and the thudding in my head reminded me I'd drank a little more than I'd planned to last night.

There was no noise in the flat. Had I dreamed it?

A gull cawed close to the window, and I needed to go to the toilet.

I got out of bed and made my way to the bathroom. My head didn't feel too bad with the movement, which was a good sign. I went to the toilet, splashed some cold water on my face and left the room. The folded piece of paper on the mat by the front door caught my eye immediately. My name was handwritten on it and looked like the note from yesterday.

Fear hit me in the stomach like a punch. I crouched down carefully, trying to keep my head steady, and picked the paper up. I opened the sheet with a growing sense of dread.

Are you scared yet? I wonder what you'll do to make
sure no one else finds out how naughty you were after
the meeting. Have you been back to the mechanics…?

I sat with my back to the wall, feeling horribly sick. The
person knew I'd done something after the meeting and,
apparently, where, which meant it had to be Freddy. He
hadn't struck me as being unpleasant or manipulative,
though I was in a heightened state of emotion when I met
him and that's never the best place to be when making a
judgement. Unless he'd been foolish enough to tell
someone else.

* * *

It took two headache tablets, a coffee, a slice of toast
and a long hot shower to make me feel better. By the time
I locked the door behind me, I was fed up of turning my
thoughts about the notes over in my head without being
able to see any kind of fresh angle.

A car engine started as I walked out of my building
and, a hundred yards or so to my right, a pale-blue Mini
pulled out and drove slowly towards me. It seemed to slow
down as it passed by and I glanced at the driver. I felt a
quick jolt of recognition and was sure it was Ogilvy, who
I'd last seen at the protest meeting.

I checked the registration plate and saw it was HK72
but knew I'd never remember the rest. I watched until the
car turned out of Marlborough Street. Could it really have
been Ogilvy and, if so, why was he on my street first thing
in the morning? Was it a coincidence or did he have
something to do with the notes? Could there be a link
between him and Freddy? Was I being paranoid or was my
life properly turning to shit for some reason?

Paranoia or not, I took a different route to work just in
case Ogilvy knew my routine and was lying in wait for me
somewhere. When I reached Norfolk Road, I stood by the
corner looking towards the Town Campus. A couple of

students were milling by the gates, vaping and laughing. A couple of cars drove by but didn't slow and neither of them were Minis.

Another car pulled up at the kerb near the junction to Fisher Lane, which led to the other campus. A young man got out, grabbed his bag then slammed the door shut. He ran his hands through his white-blond hair and looked my way.

I recognised him instantly and the sense of horror sent a chill through me. He looked younger than I remembered. It seemed to take Freddy a moment to place me and then he smiled. I glared at him and he waved.

"Hey," he called. We were a hundred yards or so apart, far enough from the campus entrance that none of the students there turned to look. And even if they did, what would they see other than a student and lecturer greeting one another?

He walked towards me and I panicked. What was he doing? After sending those notes, or being party to them, he was going to approach me in the street? What the fuck was he thinking?

I didn't have many options, but I knew I didn't want to run. Why should I inconvenience myself? I wasn't going to let him dictate how the situation played out.

With a deep breath, I walked briskly towards campus, determined not to show how uncomfortable I felt.

"Hey, Kim!" He sounded cheerful and friendly. "How're you?"

How could he be so brazen? I looked at him in disbelief as he crossed the road at an angle to intercept me.

"Kim? Aren't you speaking to me?"

"What are you doing?" I demanded without slowing my pace.

"Hey, nice to see you, too." His smile barely faltered. "How's this for a small world? I was hoping to run into you."

"Yeah, sure you were."

"Why wouldn't I?" A flicker of doubt crossed his face. "I got home on Sunday and couldn't believe I didn't get your number."

He stopped at the kerb as if expecting me to do the same but when I strode past, he quickly fell into step. "I've never met anyone on the council before and thought you had to be a certain age, so I didn't realise you were a student here, too."

That pulled me up sharp and I turned to face him. "Tell me you're kidding."

"What?" He frowned. "How was I supposed to know you attended here? If you're on this campus, and I'm on the other one? I never saw you before Sunday night."

"Freddy," I said carefully. "Do you seriously think I'm in my early twenties?" He'd only seen me under artificial light, and I wondered how old I now looked to him with the sun on my face.

"Well, no," he said tentatively, as if he didn't want to offend me. That didn't make any sense either, because how could he send me threatening notes but then not want to hurt my feelings about my age? "That's why I was surprised, what with you being on the council and everything. I saw you and it took a moment to register but then I thought you might be a mature student."

"A fucking...?" I shook my head. "How old do you think I am?"

"I don't know? Late twenties?"

"You're a gem," I said sarcastically. "Now just leave me alone." I walked away.

"Hey," he called and jogged to catch up with me. "I don't understand."

I stopped so quickly he had to backtrack. "You don't understand?" I asked, struggling to keep my voice low as my temper rose sharply. I felt the heat of it spread across my chest. "I don't either, and I hate that almost as much as I hate getting mysterious notes and being threatened. So, I tell you what. From this moment on, we don't speak to one another ever again, we hopefully never see one another again and you stop sending me sinister notes. Do you understand?"

He looked hurt but didn't say anything.

"Leave me the fuck alone, Freddy." I stalked away and, thankfully, he didn't try to follow me. I was angry now and if he'd said anything else, I might have flipped and that wouldn't have helped anything. I got through the gates, out of his sight and stopped, just to be still. I shook my hands out and stared at the ground until the blood wasn't loud as it rushed in my ears. It took a few moments before I could hear birdsong, gulls cawing and people talking. I looked towards the main building and noticed movement in George's window. He was looking at me and I wondered how long he'd been standing there. Had he seen me having words with Freddy, or watched me shaking out my anger?

Well, if he had, there wasn't a lot I could do about it.

Chapter 11

My office was a narrow room only slightly wider than the desk that sat at one end in front of the window. The filing cabinet had seen better days and three shelves held so many textbooks and reports that they bowed to an alarming degree. I'd supplied my own travel kettle.

The air felt still and stuffy, so I opened the window before I sat down. The chair squeaked as I leaned back and stared at the ceiling, thinking about Freddy Medwin and what I could do about the situation.

Someone knocked briefly on the door then it opened slightly and Adam peered around. "Hey. How's it going?"

I knew he would support me as a friend, but I was too embarrassed at my lapse in professionalism to confess all.

And speaking of professionalism, he'd be duty-bound to report what I told him, anyway. "Okay," I said. "You?"

"Not bad, considering it's Tuesday and I have several students in my first lecture so involved with their phones we could literally have a fire break out in the room and they wouldn't notice. It's one of the joys of teaching."

"Did they have mobile phones when you were at teaching college?"

He laughed sarcastically. "No, we were still on baked-bean cans tied with string. Are you up for lunch?"

"Of course."

"Great stuff." He went to go then clicked his fingers. "Oh yes, I almost forgot. I got a message that Gorgeous George wants to see me during break."

"Did he say what for?"

"No, didn't you get one?"

"I haven't checked my emails yet." I would normally have done it on my phone while I ate breakfast, but I'd been distracted during the morning.

"Maybe it's about the head of department," he said and gave me a thumbs up. "I'll see you later."

When he'd gone, I opened my laptop to check my email. There was nothing from George or his secretary and I felt a twinge of disappointment.

* * *

At lunchtime, Adam was waiting near my lecture room, and we walked outside together. Students were sitting on the grass, some on their own and others in small groups, making the most of the sunshine.

"So did you see George?" I asked. The thought of their meeting had been on my mind all morning.

"It was nothing to get excited about, more's the pity; he wanted to talk to me about something on my course. I think he was winding me up, though, because I'm sure he smirked when my interest dropped."

"That was nice of him," I said sarcastically.

"Yeah, that's what I thought."

Someone called his name. A pretty brunette with thick-rimmed glasses was coming towards us across the grass, clutching several folders to her chest. "Sorry to bother you, Adam, but can we have a moment?"

"Sure," he said to her then glanced at me. "I'll meet you there."

"No problem."

I followed the path around to the rear quad of the college. The refectory, a one-storey monstrosity from the early seventies with a lot of windows and plastic trim, was bordered on three sides by faculty buildings. At some point, a patio had been built in front of it and it was filled now with picnic tables packed with staff and students.

As I walked towards the patio, I saw someone coming towards me from the corner of my eye.

"Kim?"

I looked at Freddy and experienced the same kind of free-fall sensation you get when a big fairground ride suddenly drops you. He looked worried, and his hands were fidgeting so much he clasped them together.

"I'm sorry to do this to you," he said and sounded very apologetic. "But I needed to see you."

I glanced towards the patio but, of course, nobody was paying any attention because nothing unusual was going on, it was my paranoia making me think otherwise.

"I thought I made myself perfectly clear earlier on," I said, through gritted teeth.

"You did but that's kind of why I want to talk to you." He was bouncing on the balls of his feet, a bag of visible nervous energy.

"How did you even know I'd be here? Have you been following me?"

"No," he said. "But I thought you'd have to eat so I've been walking around the refectory trying to spot you."

"Are you insane?" My heart was thumping but my blood felt cold and I had chills across my shoulders. I couldn't believe this was happening. "Do you realise what that sounds like?" I could only be thankful he didn't realise I was a tutor otherwise he might have caught me at my office.

He pulled a face. "I'm not stalking you, or anything weird like that."

"That's what it bloody looks like," I snapped. "And now you've found me, at lunchtime, when the place is packed with people. You really do know how to pick your moments, don't you?"

"I wasn't trying to pick a moment or be an arse. I just want to get everything sorted out. I don't want you to be angry at me."

"What did you expect? You're a student, Freddy, and I'm a tutor."

"You're a…?" He looked startled and colour flushed his cheeks. "Oh, shit."

I work in a profession where casual white lies – 'I did my homework, but I forgot it' – abound and I've developed what I consider to be a fairly decent bullshit detector over the years. His reaction didn't trigger it, so either I was way off or he was being honest.

"Oh, shit, indeed."

"I didn't know that."

"And now you do, yet you're still standing there. Go away."

"I can't. I know this just makes things much worse, but I need you to understand."

"Understand what?" Bile rose in my throat. Why wouldn't he just walk away? "Freddy, I broke a major college rule and it could easily cost me my job. It's so serious, in fact, it could even hurt you."

"I genuinely didn't know you were a tutor." He took a step towards me. "It's not what you think, Kim. I need to speak to you, to straighten everything out."

He reached for my arm, but I yanked it out of his reach. "Don't touch me!" I shouted and took a step back. This was a living, breathing nightmare.

"Kim," he said, plaintively.

I was aware of someone coming up behind me. I dragged my attention away from Freddy and realised, with horror, the diners on the patio were staring at us. None of them were speaking and it felt horribly quiet. Embarrassment warmed my face and my palms were clammy.

"Go away," I said, quietly but firmly.

Adam put his hand on my shoulder. "Are you okay, Kim?" Concern was etched into his expression. I shook my head at him.

Freddy looked startled to see Adam, as if he hadn't expected any other faculty members to appear, and then his gaze settled on me. His eyes were filled with tears, and he looked like someone who'd got messed up in something he really didn't understand.

Adam let go of me and took a step towards Freddy. Freddy took a step back. "So, how's it going, mate? Are we having a problem here?"

"No," Freddy said slowly. "I don't think so."

"Are you a student here?"

I felt nauseous. If Adam asked the right question, then I was in real trouble. "He's based at the other campus," I said quickly. "It's okay, really. I think he mistook me for someone else."

"Oh, yeah?" Adam quirked an eyebrow. "Is that right?"

Freddy looked as if he wanted the ground to open up and swallow him. "Yeah. I thought she was someone else."

"Well, you're in the wrong place at the wrong time then, son," said Adam. "I think you ought to go."

Freddy looked as if he was going to say something else then blew out a breath and started towards the path. He glanced over his shoulder. "I'm so sorry," he said. "I really am."

"She knows," Adam said. "Come on, get going. I'll walk you to the gate."

"You don't need to do that."

"I really think I do," Adam said and looked from Freddy to me. His concern was intense. "Are you sure you're okay?"

"Uh-huh," I said.

Adam put his arm around me and squeezed but it didn't feel at all reassuring, and I stepped out of his embrace. He looked hurt for a moment, but I couldn't help that. I just wanted to go somewhere and hide.

"I'm fine, honestly. I'll go back to my office."

"Don't you want to get some lunch?"

I looked at the patio. Most of the diners had gone back to their food and conversations. I wondered how many were discussing what they'd just seen. Worse, I wondered if any of them had taken pictures or video. "No. I think I've lost my appetite."

"That's understandable. I'll come and see you when I've finished escorting fella-me-lad here."

"You really don't need to do that," said Freddy and walked away.

"I'll catch you later," Adam said and hurried after the student.

Chapter 12

I sat at my desk, feeling no calmer, and rubbed my eyes furiously as I tried to make sense of what had just happened. It felt like I'd half-completed a jigsaw and only now discovered that some of the parts were missing.

I was angry with Freddy for ambushing me and also with myself, for reacting badly in front of so many people to a situation I'd helped create. Adam had seen it all too and had to intervene, so now I felt as if I owed him an explanation. But what could I tell him? If I revealed everything, he'd be caught between a rock and a hard place and he might also want to know why I hadn't trusted him enough to tell him all the sordid details yesterday, when I realised what I'd done.

Guilt amplified my anger and my secret felt like a hand grenade sitting just out of reach and ready to explode.

"Shit."

My head was pounding, and I dry-swallowed a couple of tablets, hoping to chase the pain away. My fingers tingled and I flexed them. My stomach cramped and, for one awful moment, I was convinced I was going to be sick. I reached for the bin, but the sensation passed and I knew it was a reaction to the tumult of emotion I was experiencing.

But behind all of that was the niggle about Freddy himself. He absolutely shouldn't have followed or confronted me, but something about his demeanour didn't sit right. It seemed like he genuinely hadn't known I was on the faculty, so why would he be trying to blackmail me? And if he had known, why would he confront me when I could easily call him out? And what had he meant when he said this wasn't what I thought it was? Did he mean the blackmail or something else? What did we need to get sorted out?

My sense of confusion grew, and my eyes were hot with tears.

The desk phone rang. I reached for it and put the bin down. "Kim Morgan." Somehow, I managed to keep my voice steady.

"Hi, Kim, it's Helen," George's secretary said. "He wants to know if you've got a moment."

That was all I needed. "Of course. I'll be up in a minute."

* * *

I washed my face with cold water in the staff bathroom. My eyes looked horribly red in the mirror but there wasn't a lot I could do about that, so I walked to the administration block taking deep breaths and trying to calm myself down.

Helen gestured for me to knock on the door and George called me into his office straight away. I sat down and waited as he typed something. It seemed to take a while, as if he was trying to compose what he was going to say. Or perhaps he was trying to make me stew on what had happened.

"You wanted to see me?" I prompted him. I didn't have time for petty mind games.

"I did." He looked at me. "I heard about the incident at the refectory."

With that many witnesses, I wasn't surprised the news had travelled so fast. "I thought you might have."

"I need to understand what happened." He took a deep breath and let it out slowly. "Helen's trying to get hold of our HR people."

Oh no, I thought. "HR?"

"Absolutely, Kim. I simply can't have our staff terrorised on site, especially not with that Ofsted inspection due." He cleared his throat. "And, of course, I don't want you to feel uncomfortable."

"I don't feel uncomfortable, George." He couldn't have had time to speak to Freddy, so he'd either misunderstood the situation as it was explained to him, or he'd been told wrong.

"As I heard it, Freddy Medwin grabbed you and that's him off site for good."

That wasn't what I wanted at all. For a start, he hadn't grabbed me but also, if he was removed from campus, surely what we'd done on Sunday would come out. My mind was still trying to put all the pieces together and my conscience felt like it was twisting with ramifications of my actions, too.

"He reached for my arm but there was no harm done, I promise you. He said it was a case of mistaken identity and

I believe him." Technically, I wasn't telling a lie, though that was stretching the definition. My stomach cramped and I tried not to think about the repercussions if these untruths began to unravel.

George raised his eyebrows for long enough that I thought he was waiting for me to speak again before he said, "Mistaken identity?"

"What else could it be?"

"Well, now I'm worried that he might grab another student or faculty member. I really can't have that kind of thing going on."

"I understand that, George," I said, thinking on my feet. "But I'm a tutor and he's a student." It felt like the hole I was digging was getting deeper. "If he was talking to a peer, then maybe they wouldn't be so surprised and react the way I did."

He tilted his head in consideration. "Well, that would make sense. Unfortunately, his head of department met with him as Mr Medwin returned to the second campus. After a brief discussion, it was decided he'd leave site and return tomorrow for a meeting."

That didn't make me feel better.

"Everyone will have had a chance to clear their heads by then," George continued. "And hopefully, Helen will have been able to raise someone from HR."

It was getting worse. I suddenly felt hot, my skin prickly and uncomfortable as my agitation grew. Very soon, I was convinced, George would be able to see it in my face. Why was I just adding worries to my growing collection? If Freddy was interviewed and felt his college career was at stake, would he tell the truth? I knew he was in his last year, but he still wouldn't want to leave under a cloud, surely? And if he did tell the truth, that would just make me look even worse because I hadn't said anything when I'd had the chance to. I'd be sacked for sure.

"Is it necessary to involve the HR department?" I knew I was potentially making things worse, but I couldn't see any other option. "I mean, they'd surely inform the Ofsted inspector."

From the way George's face dropped, it was clear he hadn't thought about that angle. "Ah."

"If it really was a case of mistaken identity, then there's nothing to check into."

"Hmmm." He leaned forward. "Are you saying you don't want me to pursue this?"

Of course not, I wanted to scream but I paused a moment so as not to seem too eager. "I think so."

"You've surprised me, Kim." He didn't seem unsettled and even if it was the Ofsted threat that made his decision, it still felt like he'd crumbled too quickly

"Have I?" It was hard to keep my voice steady.

"Yes. I wouldn't have expected you to say that in a month of Sundays." He rubbed his hands together nervously. "The college will obviously abide by your decision but, you know, with Ofsted, you'll have to sign something."

Was that really it finished with? "I will."

"I know you will." He sounded more nervous now than when we'd started the meeting. "Why don't you take the rest of the day?"

"I have classes."

"I'll get them covered. Go home, have a quiet evening and a think, and come back tomorrow."

"I'm not going to change my mind, George."

"No, I don't think you will." He watched me as I stood up. "But I'll have that form ready for you to sign and then we can decide how we move forward."

"I'll do that, George."

"Thank you." He stood up and didn't seem to know what to do with his hands. I thought it was because he was unsure whether to shake my hand, then I realised it was nerves. "And thank you for allowing us to deal with this issue so quickly."

"You're welcome," I said and left.

Chapter 13

Adam was standing outside my office holding a takeaway cup of coffee and a wrapped sandwich. I felt a rush of affection that he'd waited for me, and his presence was a little oasis of normality in what had become an increasingly twisted day.

"Hey." He smiled hesitantly. "Helen said George had called you in. What did he say?"

"He's sent me home for the afternoon."

"That's it?"

"Isn't that enough?"

"Well, yes, unless he's saying what happened was your fault."

"No, he just wants to give me some time away. I'm back in tomorrow and have to sign a form."

"Something to protect himself against Ofsted, I suppose?"

"Something like that."

He put the cup on the floor and rested the sandwich on top of it then held his arms wide and tilted his head to one side. "Do you need a hug?"

I hadn't realised how much I needed one of his comforting hugs until then. I allowed him to pull me in tight against his broad chest and I held him as tightly as I could. It felt good, like always and, yes, there was a certain level of desire entwined with the sense of security and safety. I missed his physical presence even though I knew I'd made the right choice ending our romantic involvement. We were on different paths and some of that was the age gap, with his aims being far longer-term than mine, including starting a family. His new partner, a woman called April who lived in Lowestoft, was apparently nearer his age and their life goals were more closely attuned. I'd never met her, but she seemed to make him happy.

"Thanks," I said as he let me go. I unlocked the office door, and he handed me the coffee and sandwich as I went in. I put them on the desk and sat down. He sat in the chair opposite.

"So, what happens now?"

"I go home, like the man told me to. He said he'd cover my classes so there's not a great deal I can do here."

"And what happens about the situation with the student?"

"I think we might talk about tomorrow." I wished I could talk to Adam about it.

"So long as it gets sorted out."

"I'm sure it will. The student had me mixed me up with someone else."

"Uh-huh," he said and raised one eyebrow theatrically as if he didn't believe me. "Listen, I've only got one class this afternoon so let me have a word with a colleague and then I'll walk you home."

"You don't have to do that," I said, touched by his offer. "But if you could, that'd be lovely."

He gave me a warm smile and left the office. I drank some coffee then opened the sandwich wrapper. I took a bite of the chicken mayo, but my appetite still wasn't there, and the food had the texture and moisture content of cardboard. I managed to swallow my mouthful then rewrapped the remains of the sandwich.

Adam was back in five minutes. "Okay, whenever you're ready."

I grabbed my bag, locked the office and we left campus. He did most of the talking as we walked towards town and I listened absently to what he'd seen on television last night and how dazed a colleague was who'd just come off paternity leave. I chipped in now and then but was content to listen.

"How about a nice bottle of wine?" he asked as we passed an off-licence.

"I shouldn't really," I said. Not after waking up with a hangover this morning. "I'm not sure whether I'd be good company, anyway."

"Don't be silly," he said. "You're always good company. We don't have to drink the whole thing." He tipped me a wink and went into the shop, coming out a few minutes later with a bottle of pinot grigio. He put it in his messenger bag and we carried on walking.

"Do you think you'll get George to take things further with the student?"

"I don't think so."

"I heard him say something wasn't what you thought it was."

"That's right."

"Do you know what he meant?"

"No." That, at least, was the truth.

Adam clicked his tongue but didn't say anything and we walked in silence past the Hippodrome and crossed the road.

"I wonder if the student'll try and speak to you again?"

"I hope not." I wanted Adam to stop quizzing me. "I wouldn't worry about it."

"But what if he knows where you live?"

I looked at him sharply. "How would he know that?"

"I don't know." Adam shrugged. "I'm just thinking aloud."

We turned into Marlborough Street and a car pulled away from the kerb opposite my building and drove in the opposite direction. The number plate started HK72, and I wondered if Ogilvy had been scared off when he saw me with Adam. Had he been waiting for me to pass by so he could finish the conversation we'd started on Sunday?

We stopped outside my building and Adam stood in front of me. He was over six foot, a good six inches taller than me and when we'd been together, I'd enjoyed leaning into him and resting my head on his chest. I had to fight the temptation to do it now.

"Are you sure you're okay?" he asked and took the wine out of his bag and handed it to me.

I took it curiously. "I thought we were going to share this?"

He looked uncomfortable for a moment, and I suddenly realised he didn't want to spend the evening with me at all. I'd misread the situation. "You don't have to, of course."

"I'd love to, Kim, but I'm spending the night at April's."

"And you'll have a grand time, I'm sure," I said, trying to sound positive. I raised the bottle. "I'll be fine with this."

"Just don't drink all of it," he said then leaned down and gave me a quick peck on the cheek. He was wearing the musk aftershave that suited him so well. "I'll see you tomorrow but, in the meantime, if you need anything tonight then give me a ring."

"I will," I promised.

He held my hand for a moment then walked away. I watched him go.

Chapter 14

The flat felt warm and still, so I decided to go out and get some air. I put the wine in the kitchen, opened all the windows and changed into a vest top and shorts. I peeled off my socks, put on flip-flops and left the flat.

I made my way down to Marine Drive because I thought it might be pleasant to sit on the beach and enjoy the sea breeze. I waited for a group of Lycra-clad cyclists to go by, then crossed the road and walked towards the main pier. Toddlers ran around and splashed in the waves, supervised by parents clearly making the best of the weather. An enterprising donkey owner led a small group of steeds traipsing sullenly across the sand with excitable kids clinging on the saddles.

A group of teenagers, all of them looking like they should be in school, walked by sharing a cone of chips.

On the far side of the pier was a concrete ramp that led down to the beach. A bowling green was on the other side and a match was in full swing, with very serious-looking pensioners studying the game. None of them looked particularly happy.

The ramp ended at the walkway which bordered the beach and ran from the funfair at the southern end of Marine Drive right up to the old Holidaze holiday camp to the north. Beyond that was the marshland Brian Glover planned to build over.

I liked this part of the beach because it was quieter than the other side of the pier, where all the activities were located. There were also usually fewer people here and it felt like you could enjoy a bit of peace.

A takeaway coffee stall built into a horsebox was standing under the pier and the young woman behind the counter smiled expectantly at me. She was slim and thin-faced, with hair all the colours of a rainbow and a lot of piercings along one eyebrow. I checked the listing of drinks they offered and decided to have a cup of tea.

"This Indian summer we're having is dragging on now, isn't it?" she said as she poured the water.

"It is. At least you're in the shade."

"We goths don't like suntans."

We laughed and she handed me the cup. I paid her and we said goodbye and I walked back out into the sunshine.

I sat on the edge of the walkway and slipped off my flip-flops, burrowing my toes into the warm sand. It felt very nice. I put my hands behind me and leaned back, turning my face towards the sun. The sound of the waves mixed with the far-off shouts of the kids on the beach and the occasional cry of victory from the bowls match had a lulling effect on me. It was lovely. I sat that way for a few minutes, enjoying the bliss before I was aware of footsteps and then someone stood in my light, taking the warmth from my face.

I shielded my eyes as I sat up straight. A man towered over me, but I couldn't see his face because the sun was behind his head. It was an unpleasant sensation, and he must have known how intimidating it was.

"Can I help you?" I asked.

"Maybe," Ogilvy said.

It felt uncomfortable, after seeing him in my street, to have him turn up here. He stepped to one side and I twisted my face away as the sun blinded me. I rubbed my eyes as he walked around to stand on the other side of me. I blinked through the dark spots in my vision and looked at him.

"Do you remember me?"

"Of course I do. You spoke to me at the protest meeting, and I've seen you twice today on my street. And now, here you are, following me."

"Following you?" He gestured with both hands towards his chest, as if to say 'who, me?'. "Not at all."

I stood up and brushed the sand off the soles of my feet. "Well, that's good to know."

"You don't need to get up, Councillor Morgan."

"Oh, I think I do." I didn't want him looming over me anymore.

"It's curious we both find ourselves on the beach at the same time. Tell me, what brings you out here?"

"I wanted to clear my mind, but I agree, it is curious. Seagrave has a lot of beaches, so what are the odds we'd be in the same place at the same time?"

"More than I'd be willing to bet on." He smirked and I didn't want to be here anymore. Even if he was a constituent, I wasn't going to let someone make me feel uncomfortable.

"I'm afraid I have to be going now, Mr Ogilvy."

"That's a shame because I was hoping to have a quick word with you. If you remember, we were going to speak after the meeting on Sunday but then your protestor friends attacked Mr Glover, and the meeting finished early."

"They were hardly my friends."

"Well, they certainly weren't his, from what I could see."

I brushed the last of the sand from my feet and slipped my flip-flops back on. "I really must get going, Mr Ogilvy."

"Call me Si, please." A breeze caught his hair and pushed a lock onto his forehead. He brushed it away absently. "Can I, at least, have five minutes of your time?"

I made a show of looking at my watch. "Five minutes."

"Thank you," he said with a distinct lack of sincerity. "I wanted to discuss your standpoint on the golf course proposal."

Nothing about this felt right, but I tried to stay calm. I was sure he knew how he was making me feel and I didn't want to give him an ounce of satisfaction. It might have been that I was reading the situation wrong, and he was a concerned citizen, but I got the unsettling sense he was working to another agenda I couldn't quite figure it out. "Are you one of my constituents, Si?"

He smirked and took a step towards me. I instinctively stepped back.

"I just want to talk to you, Councillor Morgan."

"Do I take it you work for Brian Glover?"

"Not really," he said with a little shake of his head. "I'm more of an independent contractor but I have his interests at heart and I think, between us, you and I could come to some sort of agreement."

"I'm sorry, Mr Ogilvy, but this doesn't seem like something I can help you with."

He took another step closer. "I think you're being overly negative about what could be a good-quality venture for Seagrave."

There was something almost evangelical in his tone. Had Glover hired him to intimidate me into changing my vote? "I canvassed my constituents, Mr Ogilvy, and most of them agreed with my view."

"That's unfortunate if you won't allow me the chance to correct your opinion."

That took me by surprise. "Correct my opinion?" I didn't bother to hide the disdain in my tone. "That's remarkably arrogant of you, Mr Ogilvy. This conversation is over."

"That is disappointing."

"I'm sure you'll get over it. Please don't follow me anymore."

"I wouldn't do that, as I'm sure you would report it as stalking."

"If you follow me or I catch you in my street again, then I will." I turned on my heel and strode away.

"I have no idea what you're talking about," he called after me.

I kept my head down and walked briskly up the ramp and only risked a glance back when I reached the pavement. I couldn't see him, and the sense of relief made me feel a little unsteady. I leaned against a fence support until someone cheered on the bowls green and snapped me out of it.

* * *

I locked my front door, kicked off my flip-flops and went into the kitchen to open the bottle of wine. I poured a generous glass and sat at the counter and drank some.

Today hadn't started well and only got worse. How had I managed to get myself into the middle of so much shit? The notes and Freddy were bad enough but now I had some weird bloke trying to get me to change my vote. I'd experienced odd behaviour from people wanting to discuss council business with me in the past, but this was the first time I'd felt properly creeped out.

It didn't take long to finish the glass and I poured myself another one.

Chapter 15

My head felt horribly thick and foggy when I woke up.

The light in the lounge was early-morning orange. On the television, an overly cheerful woman extolled the virtues of foldable luggage.

A thumping ache settled behind my eyes when I moved my head to look at my watch. I felt nauseous and there was a bitter and vaguely metallic taste in my mouth. It was a little after seven o'clock.

I'd slept upright on the sofa after drinking the entire bottle of wine as I watched *The Devil Wears Prada*. Why had I been stupid enough to do that, especially after the night before?

Switching off the television, I pressed a hand to my forehead to hold it together and slowly got to my feet. I went to the bathroom, washed my face gently and brushed my teeth. I took two paracetamol, drank a tumbler full of water then leaned on the sink for five minutes before having another drink. It didn't make me feel better, exactly, but I did feel less like a zombie. I went into the kitchen, made a strong coffee and ate a slice of toast.

Feeling slightly better, I had a shower and questioned some of my life choices. I was a grown woman with a responsible job and knew drinking a bottle of wine wouldn't make me feel better in the long run. I needed to sort myself out.

I was getting dressed when the letterbox clattered. I went into the hall and saw the folded sheet of paper on the mat by the front door.

My heart lurched at the sight of it. It was the same handwriting but the sheet was held closed by paper clips. I opened it and another sheet dropped out.

> *I'm worried you're not taking this seriously, so here's a little more of what you don't want others to see. Keep your mouth shut and act the way I want you to, and they don't need to. I'll be in touch…*

It took me a moment to realise the second sheet of paper showed a grainy, brown-tinted CCTV image of the apron and fence from Davis Motors. There were two figures in the murk but even with the poor quality I could tell it was me and Freddy. A date and time stamp, as grainy as the rest of the image, was printed in the bottom right corner.

My temper flared. "You little fucker," I muttered, enjoying the power in the words. So, the bastard was stepping things up, was he? If I confronted him with this image, how would he try and get out of it? He certainly couldn't use the defence of me not understanding because how could I possibly think the wrong thing looking at a photograph that captured my inappropriate behaviour? And what did he mean about me not taking it seriously? I really was taking it seriously and I refused to play the victim. I'd made a mistake by not telling anyone, but I wasn't going to let him have this hold over me. If Freddy

Medwin wanted to threaten me, then I'd take ownership of the situation and turn it around on him.

* * *

The morning was warm, with a rich golden light that cast long shadows.

My headache had faded slightly but every step I took was a little reminder of it. I entertained myself with various ways I could deal with Freddy. Some were sensible, some weren't, but all of them were satisfying in one way or another. When I reached Norfolk Road, I kept an eye out for him in case he tried to surprise me again. I had a rudimentary plan that wasn't as cohesive as I'd have liked but was better than nothing.

I would approach him as if it were just a tutor-student conference on the fly so if anyone saw me, they wouldn't pay much attention. We'd go to my office and I'd lay it on the line, that I refused to be blackmailed and if he persisted then I would tell George Royston to act on his threat to expel Freddy and would come clean about what had happened. It almost certainly wouldn't end brilliantly for me, even though I would make it clear I didn't know he was a student, but it would certainly rob him of his power.

I passed a group of students who'd commandeered a bench near the bus stop. A couple of the girls had red-rimmed eyes as if they'd been crying.

"Is everything okay, ladies?" I asked.

"Uh-huh," one of them said without paying too much attention to me.

"Are you sure?"

"Yes," one of the others said, and that seemed to finish the conversation.

I went onto campus and headed straight for the English block. Adam was leaning against the wall by my office door, talking on his phone with his back to me. I couldn't help but listen to his side of the conversation as I got closer.

"I heard it on the radio this morning," he said tersely and then listened for a few moments. "Well, there's not a lot I can do about it now, is there?" He sounded annoyed. "I'm waiting to speak to her now."

I scuffed my shoe deliberately, so he knew I was there. He glanced over his shoulder and appeared startled then gave me a dead-eyed smile.

"I have to go," he said and tapped the screen. "Hey, Kim. How're you feeling?"

Was my worry about Freddy showing? "I've been better."

"I'm not surprised," he said, almost speaking over me. "Yesterday would have taxed anyone."

His eyes were flinty, but I couldn't think what might be wrong.

"How about you?" I asked. "Did last night go well?"

Now he looked startled. "What do you mean?"

"You were going to spend the night at April's."

"Oh yes, I did." He looked uncomfortable. "I'm sorry, Kim, but did you hear the news this morning?"

"No. I wasn't feeling myself this morning and didn't listen to the radio, why?"

"So, you didn't hear about the body?"

"What body?"

"The police found a young man dead somewhere on the seafront in the early hours."

"Do they know what happened?"

"No, other than they think he was mugged sometime in the evening. They're checking the CCTV."

"Have they named him? Is he a student here?"

"They haven't informed the next of kin yet, but social media is saying he is."

It's never pleasant to hear of a death but it adds a real poignancy to the situation when the person is young. I've known a few students who passed away and it casts a terrible pall over the college.

"That's terrible."

"I know. I'm sure we'll hear something else during the day." He still had that same detached expression, but his smile this time had a bit more life in it. "Meet up for lunch?"

"Uh-huh."

"Okay," he said and walked towards the stairwell.

* * *

I dealt quickly with my new work emails and had enough time to check my personal account. There was a new one from Caitlin.

> *Kim,*
>
> *I'd hoped that, after the debacle with the protest meeting, you might have made some effort to calm situations and not bring your work with the town council into disrepute. But now I hear from colleagues on the governing board that you were involved in an altercation on campus yesterday with a member of the student body. I then saw that you were photographed with the same young man on Sunday.*
>
> *As a friend, I hoped you wouldn't put me in the situation of needing to explain the rules governing your roles both as a lecturer and as a councillor, but it pains me to say it appears you're failing at both.*
>
> *I will do what I can when questions are asked at the council meeting but I wanted you to understand my concern.*
>
> *Yours,*
> *Caitlin*

I leaned back in my chair. She managed to annoy me with her tone again, but I was also frustrated that I'd put myself into this situation. I was only glad now I hadn't responded to her email from yesterday, otherwise she wouldn't have been so quick to offer her help. It was only on my second reading of the email that I registered she'd seen a photograph of me and Freddy from Sunday.

I bit the inside of my cheek, trying to process it. The photo could have come from a member of the public, or Ryan, if he'd published his. Surely she couldn't have meant the CCTV image? If she did, then why would Freddy have made good on his threat without naming his terms? Or was she the person he'd told?

The thought that Caitlin might have been sending the notes was horrible and didn't make a whole lot of sense. Yes, we had opposing views on the golf course, but we were supposed to be friends. Would she resort to blackmail to get her own way? Or was it all about unsettling me?

Students walked past my door talking loudly and pulled me out of my thoughts. I glanced at my watch and saw it was nearly time for class.

* * *

My thoughts on how to deal with Freddy and Caitlin occupied my mind through the lecture and were still there, like pebbles trapped in my shoe, as I walked back to my office.

If I was going to do things properly, it had to be face to face, though I didn't relish the prospect of confronting either of them.

Adam was outside my office again and looked less happy than he had earlier.

"You do know this isn't your office, don't you?"

He didn't look amused. "Have you got a minute?"

"I always have for you, you know that." I unlocked the door and he followed me in. "So, what's up?"

He sat in the guest chair, crossed his legs at the knee and cleared his throat. "Did you hear any news?"

"No, I've been in lectures. If there's something you know, just tell me. I'm not in the mood for suspense."

"Okay." He cleared his throat again. "With social media, it's probably all over campus by now and I wanted you to know." He tilted his head until I heard tendons creak. "The police have identified the body on the beach as Freddy Medwin."

Chapter 16

His words seemed to lose their meaning and I struggled to comprehend what he'd said even as my stomach felt like I'd swallowed a stone. I bit my lip to try and bring everything back into focus. "He was the mugging victim?"

He leaned forward to touch my arm. "Do you feel okay?"

"I'm fine," I said but I really wasn't. The mind was fogging up. "Are they sure?"

"They mentioned his name on the news. Pam's checking with the police now, just in case Seagrave Sound got it wrong, but it's gone viral over the campuses. A lot of the students must have known him."

It didn't seem possible. The shock had hit me first, but now I was overcome with a terrible sense of sadness and loss, which pushed down my anger at him. Whatever he'd done to me, I couldn't see his death as anything other than an act of cruelty; a young man whose life was snuffed out because someone wanted a few quid. I felt sick.

"This is awful," I said, the words not strong enough for what I meant.

"I know," Adam said sympathetically. "He was only twenty-three and that's no age, is it?"

"No."

"It makes you think, though." He looked pensive. "Life's here to live, Kim. We should grasp for it every day."

"Uh-huh." I know it's a common reaction when you hear of someone passing away, but it sounded like he was saying something he'd been meaning to for a long time.

My left hand was on the desk and he leaned forward to put his own hand over it. "We need to embrace everything we can." His warm touch felt comforting in so many ways and I was about to ask him for a hug when he stood up abruptly. I missed the sensation of his touch.

"I suppose this will affect the outcome of what happened yesterday," he said. "I don't mean to sound horrible, but that could be a good thing."

It did sound horrible, but I could see his point. "You put it more harshly than I would have, but I suppose it is."

"Well, whatever it was that sparked off your incident, it's clearly over now, isn't it?"

That sounded callous so I didn't respond.

Adam didn't seem to notice and glanced at his watch. "I have to get back to my office. Are you sure you're going to be alright?"

"Yes, I'm sure." I wasn't but he seemed eager to be away and I didn't want to stop him.

"I'll drop by at lunchtime."

"Okay," I said, even though eating was the last thing on my mind.

After he left, I checked the BBC website. There was nothing on the national page, so I tried to local one, but there was no mention of Freddy. I tried the Seagrave Sound page but, as usual, beyond the myriad adverts for items not associated with the town, the news page was woefully behind the times. However, at the top of the screen was a 'listen live' option so I clicked onto that.

I pressed play on the sound bar that appeared and listened to Bobby Darin singing *Beyond The Sea*. Below the bar was a timeline and I moved it back to coincide with the ten o'clock news. The report about Freddy was brief and concise. Apparently, the victim of a mugging, his body had been found early this morning by a dog walker, and the family had been informed.

I thought about that morning's note and the CCTV photograph and what he'd said to me yesterday, about things being not what I thought.

Then it hit me like a slap. I slid the timer back and listened again and the reporter said exactly what I remembered.

Freddy's body was found early this morning.

The note and photograph were delivered this morning because I'd heard the letterbox rattle.

So, it either wasn't Freddy at all or he had an accomplice. Someone else knew what I'd done that night.

Chapter 17

The students in my next class were more subdued than normal and made their way to the seats quietly. A couple smiled sadly at me and my paranoia kicked in, wondering if they were making the connection between me and Freddy after seeing us yesterday.

I started talking about *The Crucible,* but it was soon obvious they weren't taking it in. They were dealing with a bereavement and I felt that loss with them.

"How are you all, after hearing the news?" I asked.

There was a wave of murmurs and some rustling as students shifted in their seats.

"It feels odd," said Martha. She was one of my most engaged students and sat in the front row. "It's not good."

A few agreed with her.

"It's not, it's a real shame," I said. "Did any of you know him?"

A few hands went up, but they were in the minority. I understood that. You couldn't know every student on campus, but if anything happened to one of them, you felt it.

"I knew him through a friend," Martha said. "He fixed her car and we spent a Saturday morning talking with him, sitting on the pavement while he tinkered around under the bonnet." She smiled at the memory. "He seemed like a good lad."

"That's what I heard," said Michael from near the back. He rarely spoke in class.

"Did you know him?" Martha asked, looking at me intently.

"Not really," I said. The lie tasted bad and felt horribly obvious.

"It seemed like he knew you, Kim," Michael said. "I wasn't there but friends said you two had an argument by the refectory."

"It wasn't an argument, as such. We were talking at cross purposes." It wasn't quite a lie, but I was about to step off the path of truth.

"That's not what I heard," he said.

"Does it made you feel a bit odd?" asked another girl called Jess.

"I feel bad a student has passed away," I said. "I feel bad that he and I had an incident yesterday."

"Do you know what happened?" Martha asked. "The first report said it was a mugging but now they reckon there are suspicious circumstances."

I hadn't heard that new development.

"Perhaps he was attacked," said Michael.

That set off discussions between several groups.

"I don't know," I said. "None of us will know until the police have investigated."

"I hope they investigate it quickly," said Martha.

* * *

My paranoia flared as I walked across the quad and students stopped talking to glance my way. Even a couple of faculty colleagues did the same. It was uncomfortable.

To distract myself, I thought about Caitlin's email mentioning the photograph. Was it possible she meant the CCTV one? I couldn't imagine her trying to blackmail me any more than could I imagine her being in league with Freddy.

But if it wasn't her, then who else could it be? I wasn't the kind of person to have enemies, I got on well with my neighbour and had good relationships with my faculty colleagues. My ex-husband and I weren't on good terms and it seemed like I'd lost most of our friends in the divorce, but I hadn't spoken to any of them in a long time. The only thing that could possibly lead someone to have an issue with me was the golf course proposal, a thought borne out of the fact everything had turned to shit since the meeting.

Would Brian Glover get his hands dirty for someone like me? He was rich, no doubt had good lawyers and even if the vote went against him, he'd probably still get permission.

What about Ogilvy? He had links with Glover and knew where I lived but I couldn't see how he'd fit together with Freddy.

A chill brushed my shoulders in a cold caress. What if Ogilvy had hired Freddy to help me at the protest meeting? That might explain what Freddy meant when he said things weren't as I thought. Did Ogilvy arrange the thugs, knowing they would create a chaos Freddy could whisk me to safety from?

It seemed ridiculous but, at the same time, made a certain amount of sense. If thugs were chasing me, I'd accept help, but what about the rest of it? Had Ogilvy set up a honeytrap for me? How could he have known I'd be so... I wouldn't call myself easy because I wasn't and it sounded terrible, but how could they have known I'd succumb?

They couldn't, of course, but they knew I'd be in a heightened emotional state and Freddy was a handsome young man.

The theory had more holes in it than Swiss cheese, but the paranoid side of my thinking was accepting even if the rational part wasn't.

I had to steel myself to open the refectory door and, once I had, I forced myself in. The room was nearly three-quarters full and noisy with conversation and laughter, neither of which dipped with my arrival and that made me feel a little bit better.

Adam was sitting at a table on his own. He waved, pointed at something in front of him I couldn't see, then stuck up his thumbs. I took it to mean he'd already got lunch, so I weaved my way over to him. I was right. He had a cup of coffee and a ham salad in front of him and, across the table, was another cup of coffee and a chicken salad.

"Thank you," I said as I sat down and put my bag on the floor.

"No problem." He speared a lettuce leaf and ate it carefully. "How did your morning go?"

"I've had better." I ate some of my salad. "My students were more interested in poor Freddy than John Proctor and his woes."

"I can see how that would be. I'd be more interested in watching paint dry than thinking about John Proctor."

"Hey," I said with mock offence. "You don't find me casting aspersions on oxbow lakes, do you?"

"That's because oxbow lakes are cool."

"Yeah, yeah."

"Did any of them mention the incident yesterday?"

"It cropped up once or twice."

"I had the same, because some of them had seen me walk him away. A couple were quite upset at the news."

"Well, he's one of them," I said. "He's one of us. We're going to feel it." I speared a piece of chicken and ate it slowly. "Of course."

"Listen." He put his fork down. "If you have anything you need to talk about, I'm here for you. That's what best friends do."

"I just keep thinking back to the meeting. I saw someone from it yesterday, actually. I think he's been following me."

Adam's brow furrowed. "What do you mean?"

I told him about Ogilvy and his frown shifted into an expression of surprise. "He approached you when you were down by the pier?"

"Uh-huh. I know it's a public space, but the chances of him being there at the same time as me are pretty remote, wouldn't you say?"

"I would. Where were you exactly?"

"On the walkway almost in front of the bowls club."

Adam's eyebrows rose sharply. "Seriously?"

"Yes." His reaction concerned me. "Why?"

"You do realise that's where Freddy was found, don't you?"

I felt that cold chill again. "No, that wasn't on the news report I listened to."

"I think one of my students told me. He probably caught it on TikTok, rather than the BBC." He scratched the corner of his mouth with a thumbnail. "It's a weird coincidence, though, isn't it, if Freddy got attacked in the same place where you got confronted by a man who'd been following you?"

Chapter 18

My only class of the afternoon passed without incident, and I went back to my office to do some admin work and respond to emails. I dealt with a few student queries then opened my personal account and reread Caitlin's email. I decided I'd left it long enough and wrote my reply.

Caitlin

Thank you for your email. I'm disappointed you feel I'll bring the council into disrepute as that isn't my intention at all. I'm also curious about the photograph you mention. Can you clarify where you saw it?

I read it through twice to make sure there was nothing contentious then pressed send before I could change my mind.

I checked the Seagrave Facebook page, but the only mention of the meeting was about how horribly Brian Glover had been treated by hooligans. There were no photographs, so it seemed Ryan might be an option to investigate.

His card was still in my bag, and I loaded up his website and worked my way through it. Even by the incredibly high standard Pops had established, Ryan's work was excellent. The galleries were concise – landscape, seascape, people and urban – and filled with beauty, even when he was capturing parts of Seagrave that had long since passed their prime.

His photographs in the old lido at the southern end of Marine Drive, which had been shut for as long as I could remember, caught the decay and ruin so vividly it almost made them look like somewhere you wanted to go. I spent longer than I should have done staring at a sea wall that had been damaged in a storm, the plaster now covered with graffiti, the ground a ruin of bricks and plaster.

In the people section, my heart warmed at images of Pops, sitting on his balcony looking out over the town he loved, the sun catching his eyes as he smiled for the camera.

Ryan's address was at the bottom of the main page. I locked my office and set off, glad to have a positive focus for the negative energy that had been building around me all day.

* * *

Ryan's address turned out to be the tourist information centre on Peter Street, sandwiched between a dry cleaner's and a newsagent's. It was double-fronted, with one window displaying photographs, pamphlets and brochures imploring people to sample the delights of Seagrave. The other window had been given over to a community noticeboard with a lot of information on it. One flyer was about the upcoming council vote on planning permission for the golf course. Someone had written 'It's your town, make sure you support the protest!' on it in Sharpie. I was impressed.

A bell tinkled above my head as I went through the door. The room was well laid out, with old posters on the walls advertising shows and events at the Hippodrome, and a rack by the window was filled with literature of the 'What to do in Seagrave' type. A display case contained a lot of pebbles and rocks curated, according to the sign above them, by the local junior school.

A counter bisected the room and Ryan came through the door behind it. He saw me and smiled broadly.

"Hey, Kim, this is a very pleasant surprise."

"Hi. Do you know, I've lived in Seagrave for a long time, and I've never been in here before."

He gave a half-shrug. "You and a lot of others, I have to say. Though if you live here, you hardly need information on the place, do you?"

"True." I laughed. "You need to work on your sales patter."

"You're not the first person to tell me that," he said and leaned on the counter. "So, what can I do for you? I'm assuming you don't want information on the Hippodrome programme or when the next boat trip out to Seal Island is?"

"You're right. I wanted to talk to you about the protest meeting and your photographs."

"Fair enough, my laptop's in the back office. I've just put the kettle on, as well, so if you want to come through, I'll make us both a cuppa."

I almost said 'yes' instinctively but stopped myself. After what had happened so far this week, was it wise to walk into an enclosed space with a man I barely knew?

"You don't want a cuppa?" he asked, obviously mistaking my reluctance.

"No," I said, "a cuppa will be fine."

I didn't know Ryan, but Pops did, and my granddad was generally an excellent judge of character.

"We can drink it out here, if you want," Ryan said, with concern. "I don't mind bringing the laptop out."

"No, it's okay," I said. "I'll come through."

He lifted the counter flap and I went under it, then followed him into the back office. His desk was in the left corner, facing a window that overlooked a courtyard garden. Along the back wall were half a dozen green metal filing cabinets and in the centre of the room was a long table with a microfilm reader and a photograph scanner on it. A kitchen was off to the right and several framed prints were on the wall by the door.

"It's not exactly glamorous," he said and went into the kitchen. "But it pays the bills."

"It looks good," I said. "So, what led you to this?"

He leaned against the door jamb. "I did my internship at the *Seagrave Telegraph*, which is where I met your granddad. He kind of took me under his wing because, even then, the paper was cutting staff and resources. When they shifted the operation to Norwich, the offices here shut down and this job opened, so I took it and managed to save a lot of the *Telegraph* archives as well." He gestured towards the filing cabinets. "Some of it is microfiched so I got hold of the reader and a scanner to digitise the archives."

"That's impressive." Pops had often lamented that closing the paper here meant losing a lot of history.

"I do what I can, even though I know I sound like a dinosaur when I talk about it. But Seagrave has been good to me and it's a fascinating town and I think we should try to retain the history." The kettle clicked off and he went into the kitchen. "How do you like your tea?"

"Slightly lighter than a builder's brew, with no sugar."

"I can do that."

He made the drinks and brought two mugs into the room. "Did you want to sit at the desk or stay by the door?" The fact I could hear the concern in his tone made me feel safer.

"I'll sit," I said. I doubted he'd try anything, but I could throw my tea at him if he did. I sat at the desk and he leaned against the table.

"So, what did you want to know about the photographs?"

"I'm curious as to who hired you. Was it Glover?"

"No, I did it off my own bat." He rubbed his chin. "When I inherited the *Telegraph* stuff, I decided if there was a big meeting or event in town, I'd record it to add to the archive."

It made sense and sounded like a nice idea. "So did you take many pictures?"

"Probably a couple of hundred."

"Have you published any of them?"

"Not yet. The *Telegraph* wanted some when it became a newsworthy event, but I don't know how much coverage they'll give it."

"You didn't put any on your website?"

"Nope, or on the Seagrave blog I update either."

"There's a Seagrave blog?"

"There is and you can obviously tell how popular it is." He smiled grimly. "Is there a problem?"

"I don't know." I took a deep breath and exhaled slowly. "A council colleague said she'd seen a picture which didn't cast me in the best light, but I haven't seen any pictures on social media yet."

"I saw a few people taking some with their phones, but only once the fighting started."

"So has anyone asked to see your pictures?"

"Yes, two people did, which is unusual. The police were also in touch."

"What did the police want?"

"Everything I shot, since Glover was going to press charges and there was no police presence." He came over to the desk and moved the laptop towards himself. He opened his email and scanned the messages. "As for the others, the first was from Caitlin Alexander, who must be a colleague of yours."

I nodded. "Did she say why she was asking?"

"Only that she was looking for any shots that featured council officers."

"Which was basically me."

"Well, maybe." He checked the screen again. "The other person was a man called Simon Ogilvy. He's apparently a consultant for Glover Works."

"And who did he ask to see?"

"He said Glover was concerned at the lack of security at the event and wanted to bring it up at the next council meeting, so he needed to know who was there. There was something about his attitude I didn't like, so I charged him for the prints."

Now I had answers I realised I understood the situation less. It made sense for Caitlin to request pictures as it would give her ammunition, but what would Ogilvy or Glover get from them?

"Can I ask why you want to know?"

"Some weird things have happened to me since the meeting." Ryan came across as genuine as Pops said he was, and it felt okay to be telling him the truth.

"Weird in a good way, or bad?"

"Both, I think. Listen, if I tell you something, can you keep it to yourself?"

He looked surprised but held up his hand in a Scout salute then saw my expression and lowered it sheepishly. "I can."

"The thing is, it makes me sound paranoid even to myself and I don't think I am." I told him all about Sunday night, except for what happened in the garage. Laying it out in as straightforward as I could, it sounded even more paranoiac than I'd expected but his expression didn't change.

"The police were keen to see pictures of him, obviously."

"I can imagine. Did they say anything?"

"Not to me." He finished his drink. "I'd be happy to show you the pictures, if you think that'd help? I have facial-recognition software and you're in it, because of Mrs Alexander's request, so we can see yours specifically."

"That'd be great."

"Do you mind?" he asked. He gestured to the floor beside my chair and waited for me to nod before he knelt there.

He opened a program on his laptop then turned the machine slightly, so it was at a better angle for me to see. He typed my name into a search bar and the first picture appeared.

I was framed by the main door and Ryan must have been near the stage. The depth of focus blurred out a lot of the faces around me but just over my shoulder was a darker part of the shadow. I wondered if it was Ogilvy.

The next picture showed me on stage with Maureen. We were deep in conversation and it was a lovely image. The next half-dozen or so were of me on the stage and then one showed Maureen looking worried. The next few were of me guiding her off stage towards the balcony stairs. Adam appeared at the edge of one frame, his hand reaching for Maureen. Then there was a crystal-clear image of me and Freddy. It looked as if he was speaking, and I was paying rapt attention. The next photograph showed him holding my hand and the last was us going through the door behind the stage.

"That's it," Ryan said. He stood up and brushed off the knees of his trousers.

There were only three photographs of me and Freddy and I couldn't see anything suspicious in any of them. Maybe, at a push, you could make something out of him reaching for my hand but what does it show? Once the viewer is aware of the context that we're trying to get away, it shows a young man helping someone.

"I didn't realise until I went back through the pictures for the police that I'd caught you so clearly with that poor kid."

"But none of them look untoward, do they?"

"Untoward?" He sounded confused. "What do you mean by that?"

"As in inappropriate."

"Why would someone be looking for something like that?"

"To tie me in with him."

"Are you being tied in with him?"

I told him about the argument at the refectory.

"In that case, I wouldn't say there was anything untoward. He helped you out of a scuffle in a public place. If I'd realised sharing the pictures would cause you trouble, then I wouldn't have done it."

"Thank you."

"The news must have been a shock, since you only just met him. I mean, he rescues you one day and then, a few days later, he's attacked on the beach." He snapped his fingers. "Gone, just like that."

"I know." I checked my watch and stood up. "I've taken up enough of your time."

"I'm hardly overrun, Kim."

"Even so, Ryan, thank you. I appreciate this."

"I appreciate what you're doing, too, with the protest." He pointed towards the prints on the wall. "I took those on the marshland earlier this year."

I went to take a closer look. The three prints were in sequence, taken during a sunset where the reds and oranges of the sky almost glowed. In the first picture, a bird stood on a branch in the lower left corner of the frame. In the second it was mid-take-off, its wings spread impressively. The third image caught it flying away into that darkening sky.

"They're beautiful," I said.

"Thanks. The marsh warbler is pretty rare around here now, since we've lost chunks of its habitat. I was dating this woman who worked for the RSPB, and she took me out there and I fell in love with the place. If that bloody golf course goes up, we lose the bird because the development will devastate the area. I've written to the planners and the council and pitched an editorial for the paper, but everything's been ignored. I feel like the tide's against us."

"I know what you mean," I said.

Chapter 19

The blue Mini pulled out of Marlborough Street and drove towards me. Seeing it, surprised and scared me in equal measure. Ogilvy wagged a finger as if to say 'naughty, naughty' as he passed. I didn't turn to watch him drive away because I didn't want to give him the satisfaction of knowing his presence had unsettled me.

As I turned the corner, a woman stepped back from the front of my building then crossed the road towards a black Astra. She wore a dark trouser suit with a white blouse and her dark auburn hair was pulled back in a tight ponytail. I didn't recognise her.

I took my keys out of my bag as I got close to steps.

"Excuse me?" the woman called.

I glanced over my shoulder. "Do you mean me?"

"Uh-huh. You wouldn't happen to be Kim Morgan, would you?"

"I am. Can I help you?"

The woman checked both ways then crossed the road. "I hope so." She reached into her jacket and held up an opened wallet to show me her warrant card. "I'm Detective Sergeant Nina Richards and I'd like to have a word with you."

My surprise must have been obvious.

"It's only a few questions, nothing to worry about Ms Morgan. Or can I call you Kim?"

"Kim, please, Detective Sergeant.

"Ah," she said with a smile. "Only my inspector calls me that. You can call me Nina. Would it be possible to talk in your home?"

"Yes." I opened the door and we went upstairs without speaking. I unlocked the flat and went into the kitchen. "Would you like a drink?"

She stood comfortably in the doorway, at ease with herself. "Water would be fine. It's been really warm today and I seem to have spent most of it in a car with faulty air conditioning."

I put the kettle on then poured a tumbler of water and handed it to her.

"Thanks," she said and took a long drink. "Is it just you here?"

"Yes." When the kettle boiled, I made a coffee then led her into the lounge. I opened the French windows and when I turned back to the room, Nina was standing in front of my overflowing bookshelf, inspecting it like a prospective buyer checking out a new house.

"So, what can I do for you, Nina?"

"Just a few questions," she said, distractedly, checking out the spines. "Have you read all these?"

"A lot of them."

"You're well read."

"I teach English at Seagrave College, so reading's my job and my hobby."

"I thought I was a big reader, but I don't have this many books."

"People say I have too many, but I don't understand that argument. How could I have too many?"

"A lady after my own heart," she said. "Do you mind if I sit?"

"Of course."

She sat on the sofa and I sat on the chair across from her. She drank some more then put the glass on the floor. I sipped my coffee then put the mug on my desk. "What was it you wanted to ask me?"

Nina took a small notepad and pen out of her pocket and flipped it open. "I understand you were at the protest meeting on Sunday evening and witnessed the altercation?"

"That's right. Was I supposed to have reported what I saw, or something?"

"No, you weren't. Mr Glover made sure we knew all about it and Maureen Northcott from the protest group was very helpful, too."

"I'm sure she was."

"And did you know Freddy Medwin before the meeting?"

"No, I didn't."

"Even though he was a student at the college where you teach?"

"He was on the other campus."

"I saw from a photograph that he came to the stage to help you, after the group began harassing Brian Glover. What happened once you were outside?"

"The thugs chased us and we ran away from the Methodist Hall."

"I see." Nina wrote in her pad. "And after that evening, did you see Freddy again?"

I wondered how much she already knew and was just getting me to confirm. "I saw him on campus the next day."

"I thought you said he was on a different campus?"

"I did, but…" I shook my head. "I'm sorry, am I missing something here?"

She looked up from her notepad with an innocent expression. "What makes you ask that, Kim?"

"It sounded like a loaded question."

"That's an interesting word to use," she said. "No, I'm thinking particularly about the incident between you and Mr Medwin outside the refectory on your campus yesterday."

My mobile rang and she stopped talking. I didn't make a move to answer it.

"Did you want to get that?"

"I hadn't planned to," I said.

"Please. Be my guest."

I took my mobile out of my pocket. The call was from Maureen and I sent it to voicemail. "It's okay, I can take it later."

"If you're sure?" She tapped her pen against her teeth. "So, what was the incident about?"

"It was hardly an incident."

"I understand you raised your voice?"

"I did. He wanted to talk to me, but I didn't want to talk to him."

"Can I ask why?"

I bit the inside of my cheek. "Because I didn't feel it was professional."

She wrote that down. "Okay. And what were your thoughts on the protest meeting?"

The change in direction took me by surprise. "Maureen did a typically excellent job of organising it, but the actions of those thugs ruined everything."

"So you don't think those men were affiliated to the protest group?"

"I'm convinced they weren't."

"And was Freddy Medwin?"

"Not to my knowledge."

"Yet he was there that evening?"

"Perhaps he was just a concerned Seagraver."

"Maybe," she said and wrinkled her nose. "We won't know that now, will we?"

"No."

"Did you speak to him after the incident on campus?"

"No."

"How about on social media? I know there were a few TikTok videos, for instance. Did you respond to anything online?"

"No, I didn't even look."

"You weren't curious to see what had been posted?"

"I was there, Nina, I hardly wanted to watch it again.

She finished her drink. "Okay, Kim, thank you. You've been a great help."

"Are you any clearer about what happened to him? The news reports said he was mugged but I've heard now there seem to be suspicious circumstances."

"I can't speak about an ongoing investigation, especially since you're not close enough to be considered a friend or family member of Mr Medwin."

"I understand, I was just curious."

"A lot of people are," she said and stood up.

I followed her into the hall. "You can see why, though, if it's changed to being suspicious."

"Now I'm curious as to why you're so interested. Have you got *Crime and Punishment* as one of your set texts?"

Touché, I thought. "No."

Nina opened the door. "It was changed because it was unlikely to have been a mugging."

"Why?"

"Because his wallet and watch were still on him."

Chapter 20

I closed the door and felt winded.

It was awful that Freddy was dead, but the thought he'd been attacked made it all the more horrible. Was it random or premeditated? Had he been aware, when confronted, how serious the situation was? Had he suffered, or fought back when he realised there was no way out? Or, worse, had he been taken by surprise and injured before he had a chance to react?

As bad as I felt, there was also the selfish thought that I wished I'd listened to him, to find out whatever it was he wanted to tell me.

I finished my coffee, but my mind kept replaying our altercation at the refectory and I knew it wasn't likely to stop. I needed to talk to someone and rang Maureen back.

"Hello, love. How are you?"

"I'm okay," I said. Telling her about my visit from the police felt like something I should do face to face. "You?"

"Well," she said with a worried tone. "It's all a bit of a delicate situation really."

"What is? Are you in some kind of trouble?"

"It's been a long time since anyone asked me if I was in trouble, love. No, I'm not, but we need to talk and I'd rather do it in person." It sounded ominous.

"Shall I come to you?"

"Would you mind? My knee is being a right bugger in this heat."

* * *

Maureen's trim cottage had planters filled with colourful bursts of flowers on either side of the front door.

She opened it before I'd had a chance to knock. Her smile didn't cover the pain she was clearly in and, as I followed her down the hall, she had a very noticeable limp.

"You don't look comfortable, I have to say."

"It's almost like the knee needs a good oiling or something."

We went into her small lounge which was filled with memories of a life well-lived but didn't feel cluttered. Pictures were everywhere, of her and her family, of places they'd visited and good times they'd enjoyed. An overstuffed sofa and two armchairs almost filled the room and there were books stuffed into the shelving unit the television stood on.

"Would you like a drink?" she asked.

"No, but I can make you one if you want."

"I'm fine, love, but thank you."

She settled herself gently into the armchair by the window. I sat on the end of the sofa, near to her and leaned forward, my arms resting on my legs. She held her thigh and lifted her left foot onto a small stool.

"Don't get a new knee," she said and looked at me intently for a few moments. I thought she'd tell me what was troubling her but didn't.

"You said we needed to talk," I prompted.

She nodded with pursed lips. "We do." She dry-washed her hands.

"What's wrong, Maureen?" I had the horrible idea it had to do with Freddy. "Is it me? Have I done something?"

"Oh, Kim, I don't know what to say."

My stomach sank. I was right. "Say what you feel. We've known one another long enough to be honest with each other."

"You're right, we have." She cleared her throat. "You know I like you and appreciate everything you do for our group."

"I like and respect you a lot, too."

She nodded and spread her hands with a resigned sigh. "I wish I didn't have to do this because it's horrible, but I've heard things, Kim. A police officer came to see me today and I thought it was a follow-up to my report about the protest meeting, but it wasn't. She asked what happened after you escorted me to the balcony and, more specifically, wanted to know about Freddy Medwin. I didn't know he was the same young man who died on the beach last night, which is awful. Nina also said you had a very public argument with him yesterday." She swallowed loudly and looked sad. "She didn't make an explicit connection, but I have to consider how this would look to others. And that means, sadly, I need to make a very difficult and very painful decision."

I knew, with a growing sense of horror, what she was going to say. "Maureen, please…"

She held up a hand and her eyes glistened with unshed tears. "Please don't make this harder than it already is, Kim. You know I value your friendship, your guidance and your fight, but we're already up against it with Glover and his knowledge of how to spin the news. Putting something like this in front of him will be like handing the man a stick of dynamite."

I could see her point of view, but it felt like my world was slowly caving in on itself. There was warmth behind my eyes and nose. "You're right. I don't want to be a burden for you or the group."

"You're not." A tear rolled down her cheek when she blinked. She wiped it away discreetly. "I'm so sorry to have to do this, Kim, but…"

"You have no other choice?"

"I don't think so." Maureen shook her head gently. "Thank you for taking it so well."

She looked so sad that I knew I had to tell her everything. If I kept it to myself and the blackmailer delivered on their threat, she'd know I hadn't trusted her with the truth. The thought of confessing scared me, but not as much as keeping quiet did. "Let me tell you what happened." Nerves made my voice tremble while I told her the events of Sunday night in detail.

Her eyes widened when I mentioned what happened at the garage, but she didn't say anything.

"I promise you; I didn't know he was a student." I needed her to understand it was a simple, human mistake. "It was a horrible shock when I saw him on campus the next day. Then, the day after that, he approached me and tried to tell me something, but I shut him down and told him to go away. That was the argument you were told about. I didn't handle it at all well."

"I can imagine."

"So that's it." I couldn't read her expression. "I can't change what happened, however much I wish I could. And now, because he was attacked on the beach, I'm being asked questions by the police."

"Have you told them your side of the story?"

I shook my head. "I've only told you and if I say anything to the police now, it's too late. Even if he'd agreed it was consensual, I'd still have to be dealt with. I crossed a big personal and professional boundary that night. The rules are very strict."

"Oh, Kim," she said.

"And they'd ask why I didn't say something earlier, because now it'll just seem like I was trying to cover it up before." I still couldn't read her expression. "Have I disappointed you?"

"You've surprised me," she said frankly, "but I'm not disappointed. I came of age in the sixties, so I know what it's like to be young and get carried away. But, unfortunately, this only strengthens my resolve on my decision."

"I understand," I said. It hurt.

"So, what are you going to do now?"

"I don't know." I sighed. "I'm in a mess, Maureen. My life's coming apart."

"It might feel like that," she said softly and put a hand over mine, "but it's only a moment in time. All things pass, love, it's the way of the world. Keep your head and keep moving forward."

Chapter 21

I walked home and felt like worry was pressing onto my shoulders.

A Range Rover Evoque braked sharply as it passed me then pulled in at a sharp angle between two cars, its back end sticking out into the road. The passenger window rolled down.

"Kim?"

I walked towards the car. A young girl was sitting in the back and looking intently at me. Caitlin leaned over the passenger seat as much as her seatbelt would allow and smiled.

"Hi," I said.

"Hello, this is a lucky coincidence. I thought it'd be better if we talked rather than kept emailing and here you are. Have you got five minutes?"

I looked at the young girl and then the angle Caitlin had parked at. "I have."

"Excellent. There's a park a little bit down the road, I'll meet you there."

She pulled away and I walked to the corner of the street. Caitlin squeezed her Evoque between two cars and got out. She was wearing pale jodhpurs and a white blouse with a thick black band keeping her hair off her face. Her hands were on the shoulders of the young girl, who wore black jodhpurs and a T-shirt with 'Seagrave Dance' written on it.

"Hi, Kim, this is Milly."

"Hello, Milly," I said. The girl was perhaps ten and smiled shyly at me.

"I'm dropping Milly off after her lesson, but I said I needed to talk to you and that she could go in the park for five minutes. Are you okay with that?"

"Sure," I said. Milly's presence suggested this wasn't staged and I thought it would be a good chance to try and find out what was going on. "After all, notes never work, do they?"

Caitlin didn't react to my use of the word 'note' and we walked to the park entrance with Milly between us. Once she was into the park, the young girl took off like a rocket and raced to the swings. Caitlin raised her eyebrows at me as if to say 'kids…'

"We'll walk," she said and set off.

The park was a couple of hundred yards long and rectangular-shaped, bordered at the back and on one side by houses. A path enclosed a small play area and a patch of grass.

An older man snoozed on one of the benches, a newspaper opened on his lap, a Border collie asleep at his feet.

"I think we need to clear the air," she said. "We're both strong women, working in a very male environment and we should support one another. I'm concerned that maybe you feel that didn't come across in my emails."

I might have gone out of my way to smooth things out in the past but now I wasn't in the mood. "They were harshly worded."

Caitlin looked like she wasn't used to people agreeing when she admitted to being in the wrong. "You're right and saying you were bringing the council into disrepute might not have been helpful. But you must see it from my side. I'm going to be mayor in the next term, and I need to make sure my councillors are a strong group of people with integrity."

"I have integrity."

"I know but look at the optics. You were seen by a lot of people arguing with a young man later found dead on the beach. Plus, he assisted you at the protest meeting where Brian Glover was attacked."

"And we discussed this, Caitlin."

"But when he says it on the news, who do you believe?"

"The protest group."

"Of course you do, because you're biased to Maureen."

"And you're biased to Glover."

"I hardly think that's fair. You make it sound like I've been swayed."

"That's what you've just accused me of being."

"Nonsense," she said with a dismissive wave. "We're at cross purposes here, Kim. Like I said, I want to clear the air between us. I respect you."

"Do you?"

"Of course I do, and I know you've been under stress recently."

"Your notes didn't help with that."

"My notes?" Her questioning expression looked genuine. "Do you mean my emails?"

"The ones about Freddy."

"I didn't email you about him, did I?"

"You did." Was she really this good an actress? "When you wrote that you'd seen me in a photograph. That worried me."

"Why would it worry you?" She sounded sincere. Had I made a mistake? "As befits my position in the community, I find it helps to have points of contact in various areas."

I didn't expect her to admit outright to sending me the CCTV image, but I watched her closely and there wasn't even a flicker that I'd struck a nerve or caught her out.

"Ryan told me you'd requested the pictures from him."

"I need to be thorough, Kim. Do I take it from your tone you don't think I should have?"

The steely edge to her voice made her naked question feel loaded. Not only did I get the sense she wasn't talking about the blackmail notes, but it felt like I was suddenly standing on uneven ground. "I'm surprised you needed to."

"And did you ever stop to consider, for a moment, that this might not be about you? Several councillors hadn't indicated which way they were going to vote, and I wanted to see what their intentions were. As much as you can be a pain in my backside, I knew which way you leaned."

"So, what were you going to do if you found out people were at the meeting?"

"Nothing immediately but information is a commodity, Kim, and I need to have as much as possible. I want to serve my community and I see that drive in you and wouldn't want it compromised."

"Wait, who's going to compromise me? You? Glover?"

"Me? What would I gain from that? I meant your position being compromised. I assume Medwin and your fracas with him on campus was what DS Richards spoke to you about."

It was my turn to be surprised. "How did you know about that?"

"Did you think I wouldn't?" It was a statement, not a question, and I felt the ground shift again. "So, am I correct?"

"Yes." If she had contacts, there was no point in obfuscating. "She's investigating the attack and wanted to know my link to him. She seemed satisfied with my explanation, unless you know differently?"

"I don't, I'm just trying to establish the facts."

We'd reached the entrance again. Milly was swinging herself high and watching us. Caitlin gave her a wave. "One more lap," she said, and Milly stuck up a thumb.

I didn't want to do another lap of the park. The conversation so far had disorientated me and if I'd made a mistake about Caitlin then I was no nearer to knowing who was sending the notes.

"Have you told Maureen about the police interest?"

"I have and we've agreed that I should step away from the protest group."

"You're not part of it anymore?"

"No. I think it's for the best."

"I think you're right," she said with a firm nod. "I appreciate you stood by your views, but the development will be good for our community. And it could be a benefit in disguise."

It hurt that she seemed to regard my stepping down as if it was nothing. "In what way?"

"A big project needs investors, Kim, and you could be part of it. I've already signed up for the early-bird package."

"You're an investor?" I wouldn't have been more surprised if she'd slapped me.

"Why not? I understand investing isn't for everyone, but if you have the courage and the funds for it, it can work well for you."

I held her arm to stop her. She looked at my hand with disdain then at my face.

"I'm sorry, Caitlin." My temper was rising and I needed to make sure I understood. "Are you saying I should vote for the proposal because there's an opportunity to make some money?"

"Why are you phrasing it like that?"

"What?" I wasn't the only one crossing boundaries, it seemed.

"This," she said and shook my hand off. "Getting all uppity."

"Caitlin, you can't vote for something you're going to directly benefit from."

"What're you talking about? Seagrave as a whole will benefit, even if it's just a reduction on the council tax from the increase in revenue Brian will generate for us."

"But the money will go to you."

"Oh, grow up, Kim, this isn't against the law. It's an early-bird investment package, open to everyone from big City firms to me, you and that man asleep on the bench."

"And does he know about it?"

"How the hell should I know?"

"I never knew about it."

"It didn't seem worth telling you, since you were dead set against it. I've given a lot to this community over the years and so has Brian. We're not Johnny-come-latelies swooping in to asset-strip the place." We'd reached the swings and she gestured for Milly to come over to us. "I wanted to clear the air, Kim, and I hope we have, even if we're still not on the same page."

"No, we're not."

"What else do you want me to say, Kim?" She looked like she wished this conversation had never taken place.

"Nothing."

Milly regarded us curiously, as if aware of the atmosphere but not sure whether she should mention it. "Are we going now?" she asked.

"Sure," said Caitlin. She took the girl's hand. "Say goodbye to Kim."

"See ya," said Milly.

Chapter 22

My mobile rang as I walked away from the park in the gathering twilight. Adam's face was on the screen.

"Where are you?" He sounded worried. "I've been looking for you since I got out of work. I wanted to make sure you were okay."

"I'm fine."

"But you're not home because I'm outside your building and you haven't been answering your buzzer."

"I went to see Maureen and then Caitlin Alexander just caught me."

"Caitlin who?"

"She's a colleague of mine from the council."

"Sounds like you've had a lovely afternoon."

"It hasn't been my best."

"Are you heading home now?"

"Yes." It'd be nice to see a friendly face and the distraction might be what I needed to try and settle the jumble of my thoughts. The ground, it seemed, was shifting in a lot of aspects of my life.

"I thought we could grab a bite to eat. My treat and you choose the food."

"I don't really fancy eating out," I said. I didn't want to risk running into Caitin again, either. "Anyway, aren't you seeing April tonight?"

"I can't go every night."

"It's your age," I said, unable to resist. "It apparently happens to most men in their middle age."

"For starters, that's not what I meant, and for seconds, I'm only barely into my middle age."

"I think the word 'barely' is pushing it a bit, to be honest."

"Yeah, okay, kiddywink. So how about I cook? We can go to mine and have a drink and a natter. It'll be an oasis of calm after your crappy day."

He was right. "I'll be home in about five minutes."

* * *

"I thought I could rustle up some of my world-famous spag bol," Adam said as he pulled out of Marlborough Street.

"That'd be nice." While I wasn't the world's greatest cook, I quickly discovered when we were a couple that he was even more hapless than me. He blamed it on his ex-wife who, apparently, was such a great cook he hadn't bothered to compete. I taught him some basic dishes and the one he latched onto was spaghetti bolognaise.

"Did you want to talk about Maureen and your lady from the council?"

"Not really. How was your day?"

"It could have gone better, but probably for different reasons to yours."

Adam drove through town to a small housing estate on the Radnor Road. His divorce settlement wiped him out and he'd ended up in a starter home he said was big enough for him but wasn't much larger than my flat.

He parked and we went into his house. After he put the post on the stairs, we went into the kitchen, and he switched on the hob then washed his hands. He got some minced meat from the freezer and put it into a pan. "Can you do the pasta?" he asked.

I half-filled a saucepan with water and put it on to boil.

He worked with an economy of movement I enjoyed watching. When the meat was browning, I took some pasta out of his spaghetti pot and laid it into the water.

"Why don't you open a bottle of wine? You know where it is."

His wine rack was in a thin alcove by the sink and filled with pinot grigio. I uncorked a bottle to let it breathe.

"Almost done," Adam said, adding some garlic and herbs. "Did you want to set the table?"

The dining room was at the back with the table in front of the patio doors. Through the glass I could see the multi-coloured fairy lights I'd bought and hung on his back fence.

I poured the wine when I went back to the kitchen and watched him finalise dinner. It smelled glorious and my stomach rumbled.

He plated the food and carried it through to the dining room. We sat down and raised glasses. "To good friends," he said.

"To good friends."

The meal was lovely and we ate in companionable silence. He refilled our glasses at one point, even though he'd barely touched his.

When we'd finished, I leaned back in my chair and ran a hand over my belly. "That was delicious, thank you."

"No problem. The spaghetti was cooked to perfection."

"All I did was put it in the water."

"Expert preparation," he said and smiled.

"Something like that."

His attentive gaze made it seem as if he wanted to say something but didn't. I looked away and covered it by having a drink, even though I was determined to slow down after the last few days.

"So, what happened with Maureen?"

I told him about stepping down.

"Well, that's hardly fair, since it wasn't your fault he had a meltdown on campus." He topped up our glasses. "Are you happy about it?"

"No, but it's probably wise, especially since I had a visit from the police."

"Eh? What did they want with you?"

"It was a mixture of Freddy and the meeting."

"Wow." He ran a hand through his hair. I'm sure it was an unconscious gesture, but I'd always found it mildly erotic and it gave me a warm feeling in my belly. I looked towards the patio because, while it might have been the wine, the last thing I needed was to get turned on by Adam, not least because he had a girlfriend.

"Yes, it's all go here," I said.

"Sounds like it." He gathered up the plates and cutlery and took them into the kitchen. "Why don't you go onto the patio while I load up the dishwasher."

I took our glasses out into the warm night and put them on the bistro table. The fresh air made me feel a little light-headed and I sat on one of the metal chairs. Surely, I hadn't drunk enough to feel tipsy?

Adam came out and sat beside me, holding the bottle. It was a little more than half full, so I hadn't drunk too much. He gestured to my glass. I shook my head, but he topped me up anyway then charged his own glass.

"George called me into his office this afternoon to talk about the head of department role," he said.

"Did he?" I felt a little twist in my sternum. "In a good way?"

"He wanted to know my plans, if I were to be successful."

"Well, that's a good thing, surely? What did you say?"

"I'm not going to tell you that," he said and laughed. "We're in competition."

I couldn't tell if he was being deliberately annoying or if I was tipsily reading too much into it. "Do you think I'd rip off your ideas?" We'd made a pact that whichever of us got the position would help the other and this felt like he was already reneging on that.

"No way." He held up his hands in an 'I surrender' gesture. "I just meant we need to go in with our own plans."

"I have my own plans."

"So, what are they?"

"Nope, that works both ways." I wagged my finger at him. I was fed up with talking about work. "Anyway, how's the romance going?"

"It's going okay," he said, though he didn't sound too excited.

"You're not giving me much information here."

"I know." He refilled my glass.

"No more, please," I said. "My head already feels like it's starting to swim." If George was going to speak to me tomorrow, then I'd need to be sharp.

"What do you mean? You're made of stronger stuff than that, Kim. We've only just had half a bottle." He held it up so I could see then refilled his own glass.

"Is that your way to change the subject from April?"

"I don't know what you mean."

"You're playing her very close to your chest. I mean, when am I going to meet her?"

"I don't know," he said with a half-shrug. "I'd like you to, obviously, but I don't want to hurt your feelings."

His sweetness was touching. "You won't hurt my feelings, Adam."

"But you're still single."

"And I'm happy with that, like I'm happy seeing you loved up."

"That's very nice of you, but aren't there any eligible young men on the horizon?"

"Nope."

"How can that be possible? A pretty young woman like you should be fending blokes off with a stick."

A blush warmed my cheeks. "Don't, you'll embarrass me."

"Perhaps I just want to make you feel better," he said with a lazy smile.

He ran a hand through his hair again and I felt that same pleasant twinge, more strongly this time. I needed to leave before I made a fool of myself. "I should go." I looked at my watch but didn't register the time. "I need my beauty sleep if George is going to talk to me tomorrow."

"You're plenty beautiful," he said.

"And you're a flatterer." I got up a little too quickly and felt giddy for a moment.

"Are you okay?"

"I'm fine."

"Well, I've had as much to drink as you, so I can't drive. Why don't you stay over? You have my bed, I'll take the sofa."

It didn't sound like a good idea. "No, a walk in the night air will do me good."

"I'm hardly going to let you walk halfway across Seagrave in the state you're in. I'll call a taxi."

"You don't need to do that."

He stood up and I don't know if I lost my balance or stepped on something that gave way under my foot but, suddenly, I was lurching forward. He moved to catch me and I fell into his arms.

"You're more subtle than you used to be," he said and laughed.

I laughed too.

He shifted position and his hand moved across my left breast. I expected him to apologise or laugh but he didn't. I liked the feel of it but it was wrong. We looked into each other's eyes.

"Are you sure you're okay?" His voice had a husky tone.

"I think so. Sorry I fell on you, but you can take your hand off my boob now."

"Oh! I didn't realise." He didn't move his hand. "Sorry."

Why hadn't he moved it? I put my hand over his, meaning to pull it away but he tilted my chin up with his finger.

He kissed me gently on the lips, or did he respond to me kissing him? Whichever it was, I knew it had to stop. I pushed against his chest and his hand fell away from my breast.

"I'm sorry," I said. "I didn't mean to fall onto you, but this isn't a good idea."

"You're right." He wiped the corners of his mouth then ran a hand through his hair again. This time it made me feel a little nauseous. "I'll call a taxi."

"Yes," I said. I sucked on my lips. What had I done?

He went into the dining room and I heard him tell someone our addresses. I stayed where I was because it

110

seemed like the best option. He came back outside when he'd finished.

"You look a bit grey, Kim. You normally handle your booze better than this."

"I'm fine." Was I? Had I really fallen or done it deliberately to make contact with Adam? We'd had one bottle between us and he was right, I normally held my alcohol better. The more I tried to figure it out, the more it hurt my head. "I'm sorry about what happened."

"Don't worry about it. People stumble all the time."

Was he pretending nothing happened to protect our friendship against my actions, or because he was right? If he was, I was only going to make things worse by talking.

"If you're sure," I said.

"Of course I am. The despatcher said the cab'll be here in a few minutes. Shall we wait in the house?"

"Yeah, that would be good."

He closed the patio doors behind me and I stood by the dining table and felt like a horrible person. We'd only just been talking about his girlfriend and then... But no, I'd stumbled. I was sure I had. I fell into him, yes, but it wasn't intentional.

A horn sounded. "That must be them," he said.

We went into the hall and I put my shoes on while he opened the door. The taxi was idling at the kerb.

"Thanks for tonight," I said. "The food was lovely."

"You're always welcome, you know that." He held my shoulder and looked intently at me. "I'll see you tomorrow."

"You will." I walked to the taxi and got in.

"Evening, love," said the driver as he expertly did a three-point turn. "Have a nice night of it?"

"I think so," I said and waved to Adam as we drove away.

Chapter 23

I still felt a bit fuzzy when I got home so I went into the kitchen and drank a tall glass of water straight down. The oven clock read as ten thirty-five, but it felt much later. I went for a shower and had it as cool as I could stand.

It was almost eleven thirty by the time I sat with my bare feet on the railing of the Juliet balcony, nursing a strong cup of coffee. While it meant I probably wouldn't sleep properly, I needed to clear my head. The ache was still there, as if it had taken up residence for the night.

I massaged the bridge of my nose then gently rubbed my eyes. How could I feel like this? Adam hadn't kept up with my consumption, but he wasn't that far behind and the bottle was nowhere near dead when we were on the patio.

So why did I feel like I'd had more?

What if I had? The horrible thought sent a chill down to my feet and I wiggled my toes at the sky. Was the bottle he brought out to the patio the one we started with? There were plenty in the rack and he could have easily drained one bottle at the table, before bringing out a fresh one. He was topping me up quicker than himself anyway.

No, that was ridiculous and a sure sign my paranoia was taking control. Why would Adam, of all people, do that to me? Did I suspect him as a way of dealing with what I'd done on the patio?

My memory of it was already starting to fuzz a little, like an old radio not properly tuned to a station, but the shame burned. Had he made a move on me, or had I made a move on him and then reacted badly when he didn't respond? Why would I even have done that when, after the incident with Freddy, sex was far from the forefront of my mind?

Trying to corral my thoughts made my head ache even more. Adam wouldn't try to get me drunk and seduce me because that didn't make sense. I was already worrying enough about the notes, Caitlin's behaviour and Ogilvy, I didn't need to be adding an innocent Adam to that list.

"This is stupid," I said. I needed to pull out of this negative tailspin and get some sleep to clear my mind.

I left the coffee, brushed my teeth and went to bed.

I barely slept.

Chapter 24

I woke up with a vague headache and a sense of shame as I remembered flashes of last night. Worrying I might have hurt our friendship, I checked my mobile but there were no texts or messages from Adam. Surely, if we'd done something stupid, then he would have tried calling this morning to sort things out. Unless he didn't want to speak to me anymore?

That horrible idea made me shudder. I got up and went out into the hallway and my stomach dropped when I saw the folded paper. I groaned, but knew I had to deal with it, so picked it up and went into the kitchen.

> *If the police are sniffing around then they're going to be very interested in what I have to say, aren't they? You know the score, Kim. Step back and keep your mouth shut, or I'll be forced to open mine and tell all.*

I tasted bile and took a few deep breaths until it passed, then reread it, annoyed that someone could play around with me like this. Why couldn't they just come out and say what they wanted? What did they need me to keep my mouth shut about?

I made a coffee and tried to think things through rationally. The only person who knew everything was Maureen and I'd told her and Adam about the police. Caitlin hadn't been at the meeting but knew I'd left with Freddy and that DS Richards had spoken to me. She might want me to keep quiet about her investment, but I wasn't aware of it until yesterday. That left Ogilvy, who'd been there that night and saw me leave with Freddy. He also knew where I lived and was following me.

My head ached for different reasons now and I hated feeling so vulnerable.

* * *

Adam rang as I walked to work.

"Hey," I said guardedly, not sure how he was going to be.

"Hi," he said brightly. "How're you feeling this morning?"

"I've got a bit of a headache."

"Yeah, I don't know what I was thinking, breaking out the wine on a school night, but you normally handle your booze well."

I frowned at the apparent insult.

"Well, that came out wrong," he said, as if he could see my expression.

"How much did we drink?"

"About a bottle between us. I should have put it away after dinner, because it looked like it was hitting you, but I didn't. So I'm sorry."

"I'm old enough to make my own decisions," I said. "I didn't do anything stupid, did I?"

"In what way?" he asked cautiously.

"Well, did I…?" We were good friends, but shame draped over me like a heavy cloak. "Did I embarrass myself?"

"No." He chuckled. "Not at all."

Had I imagined the kiss and the grope? "Are you sure?"

"Yes, I'm sure. I was there, Kim. We're friends and trust one another and I should have switched us to coffee, especially if George is going to see you today."

That shot a little charge through me. "He's seeing me today?"

"Well, I don't know for sure," he said. "But like I said to you, we talked yesterday so it'd make sense."

I had a vague memory of Adam telling me but couldn't remember it clearly.

"Are you sure you're okay?"

"I think so. I had a strong coffee and some water last night."

He laughed. "Did you sleep?"

"Not particularly well. But the fresh air's doing me some good. I'll be fine."

"Of course you will be. I'll see you at work."

* * *

DS Richards was sitting in the English block reception area and didn't look happy. She stood up when she saw me and smoothed her trouser suit over her thighs.

"Good morning, Kim. The lady on the main reception told me to wait here for you."

"That's fine. I didn't know you were coming in today."

"Neither did I," she said with a tight, cold smile. "Can I have a quick word please?"

I checked my watch. "I have a class in twenty minutes, but I'd be happy to talk before then. Did you want to come through to my office?"

"Yes," she said and followed me.

Her heels clacked on the parquet flooring and neither of us attempted conversation. I unlocked the door and opened it for her to go through. I was about to follow when George called my name.

I turned to see him walking briskly towards me.

"Morning, George. Can I get back to you? I have a visitor."

"I saw, when she signed in." He stopped and leaned in close as if he wanted our conversation to be confidential. "Is there something I need to know?"

"I would hope not, but I can't say. She was waiting for me in the foyer. I don't know what she wants."

"Quite." He glanced towards my open door. "Please update me when you're done."

DS Richards came into the corridor. "I hope I haven't caused an issue?"

"No," said George and held out his hand. "I'm George Royston, vice-principal of the college."

"Pleased to meet you, Mr Royston," she said as they shook then introduced herself. "I hope you don't mind me borrowing one of your faculty members for a brief chat?"

"Of course not, we're always happy to help."

"That's what I'd hoped," she said. "Please excuse me, it's going to be a busy day and I need to get on."

"Yes, yes," said George and looked horribly uncomfortable. "I'll leave you to it."

He walked away as I went into my office and sat behind my desk. She sat across from me.

"Excuse the mess," I said.

She looked around. "You haven't been anywhere near my desk, clearly. This is a tidy space."

I wondered how chaotic her workspace must be. "What can I do for you, DS Richards?"

"Nina, please."

"Nina," I corrected myself. "I haven't thought of anything new since yesterday."

"That's okay, I just have a couple more questions to ask you." She took out her notepad and read something then fixed me with her full attention. "You told me yesterday you didn't know Freddy Medwin before the protest meeting or why he was there."

"That's right."

"You didn't ask him about it on the two occasions you saw him on Tuesday?"

"No."

"What did you talk about the first time you saw him then?"

My mind went blank, and I tried to remember if we'd even talked about that. What had I told her? "He wanted to say hello and make sure I was okay after what happened."

"Uh-huh." She wrote something down. "Would you characterise that as a friendly conversation?"

Had anyone seen us? "I was annoyed he'd approached me at the college."

"Why? Surely that would be natural. I mean, where else would he contact you?"

Shit, I thought. I was falling further into the mess every time. "It didn't seem like a good idea."

"Why?"

"Because I've been made aware I shouldn't associate the protest group with the college."

"By your principal?"

"Yes."

She flicked back a couple of pages in her notebook. "Someone reported hearing him say at the refectory, 'This isn't what you think'." She looked at me. "What did you think, Kim?"

I met her gaze and tried to keep my breathing steady. The stress made me feel hot and sweat trickled down my back. "I didn't know what he meant." That, at least, was the truth. "Perhaps he thought I was suspicious of the fact he was at the meeting."

"Why would he think that?"

"I don't know, Nina, because he didn't get the opportunity to say."

"And that would be because your colleague…" She checked her notebook again. "Adam intervened?"

"Yes."

She tapped her pen against her teeth. "I just have one more question about Mr Medwin. It might be nothing but I need to understand the circumstances."

It felt like I'd swallowed a brick and my airway was clogged. Had my blackmailer sent her the CCTV photograph, too? "Okay."

"The area of the beach where Mr Medwin was found is covered by CCTV coverage."

"So, you saw who did it?"

"Unfortunately not. The lighting there is, frankly, terrible and the pathway isn't the focal point of the camera. However, the secretary of the bowls club, which owns the CCTV camera, was extremely disturbed by news of the attack and when he realised there was visual evidence, he forwarded it to us."

I felt a wave of relief. She hadn't seen the photograph. "And you saw me on it?"

"We did. Can I ask why you were there on Tuesday afternoon?"

"I like that part of the beach because it's peaceful. George – my principal – had given me the afternoon off and I wanted to clear my head, so I went for a walk. I had a coffee and sat with my feet in the sand."

"I saw, and it made me curious."

"Why? I often walk along there."

"Did you go back later?"

A fresh bead of sweat trickled down my back. "Are you insinuating I attacked Freddy?"

"Not at all," Nina said. "There's something here, I can feel it, but I'm not insinuating anything. So where did you go after you left the beach?"

"Straight home, where I had a drink and went to bed."

"Was anyone at home with you?"

"No, I live on my own. You know that." It felt like a cold hand had closed around my heart. "Am I under suspicion?"

"No more than anyone else who had links to Mr Medwin."

"Do you think he was attacked by someone he knew?"

"We're trying to understand if it was random or not. Perhaps Mr Medwin knew something and someone didn't want him to tell anyone."

"Like what?" If the cold hand gripped tighter, I was sure I'd have a heart attack.

"I'm just making suppositions, Kim." She shrugged and glanced at her watch. "I just have one more question before I leave you to go to your class."

I checked my own watch. I had about five minutes before I needed to make a move. "No problem."

"While you were at the beach a man approached and engaged you in conversation. Your body language, if you don't mind me saying, seemed very guarded."

"Yes. His name is Simon Ogilvy. I met him at the protest meeting, too."

"That was a busy night for you, wasn't it?"

I didn't rise to that. "He followed me to the beach on Tuesday but I've seen him a few times since the meeting, but randomly, like on my street and driving by. He was there the first time I met you."

She frowned. "That's curious, too."

"What do you mean?"

She pulled her lips down in a shrug. "Perhaps curious is the wrong word. If you see him again, though, perhaps you could give me a call." She took a business card out of her wallet, put it on the desk and pushed it towards me with her fingertips. It had her mobile number and email on it.

"I know you have a class," she said as she stood up, "but could you quickly describe him to me?"

"Why do you need me to describe him? Surely the CCTV image was clear enough in the daylight?"

"You'd think so," she said. "But Mr Ogilvy managed to keep his back to the camera all the time."

Chapter 25

I got a WhatsApp message from George as I left the lecture room. I'd spent the class in a distracted blur, wondering why Ogilvy had avoided being on camera.

Have you forgotten?

"Bollocks." I rushed along to the administration block and up to the first-floor offices.

Pam smiled when she saw me. "Hello, Kim. You look a bit stressed."

"It's been that kind of day. I went straight to my class and forgot all about George."

"Well take a seat here. Helen's away today and he's got Adam in with him at the moment."

"Oh." Had he come to a decision about the head of department? I sat in one of the guest chairs alongside Pam's desk.

"Did you get everything sorted out with the police?" she asked, leaning towards me so as not to raise her voice.

"I think so."

"Don't tell me if it's personal," she said, "but was it about Freddy Medwin?"

"Uh-huh." I was tempted to say it was personal, but then it would look like I was trying to hide something.

"I thought so," she said and nodded her head. "It's very sad. I mean, it's never nice when someone you know dies, but when they're young and with their whole life ahead of them, it seems so pointless. I mean, people get mugged and walk away from it all the time. Someone mugged my Dave once, when he was in London, and Dave just handed over his wallet and the bloke ran away. Why couldn't that have happened with Freddy?"

"I don't know, Pam."

She leaned in closer. "Can I ask you a question?"

I didn't want her to ask me anything. "Sure."

"The day before you two had that little contretemps by the refectory…"

"It wasn't a contretemps," I said quietly.

"Oh. Well, the day before, you asked to see his file. What were you looking for?"

"Nothing specific but I'd seen him at the protest meeting and then, through Adam, discovered he was a student here." It was close enough to the truth that Adam would corroborate it if Pam asked him.

"Well, that makes sense," she said. "Somebody said he helped you at the meeting."

"He did."

Her phone rang and she pushed herself back from the edge of the desk. "It's such a waste."

"It is."

It felt like a long time before George's door opened and Adam came through. He was smiling and didn't see me at first, then our eyes locked and he seemed surprised to see me. George followed him out of the office.

"Ah, Kim," he said. "Glad you could make it." There was more than a hint of sarcasm. "Thanks for coming up, Adam."

"No problem," Adam said and they shook hands. He glanced at me briefly then left.

George came over to Pam's desk. "Anything for me?" he asked even though she was still on the phone and looking at the screen.

She shook her head without looking at him.

"Come through, Kim," he said, and we went into his office. "Close the door."

I suddenly felt nervous. I closed the door as he sat at his desk.

"Sit down, Kim."

I sat and crossed my legs so they didn't jump with nerves.

"Is everything alright?" he asked.

"Yes, why?"

"Because you look a little…" He shrugged. "Did you get everything sorted with the police?"

"I did, thank you."

"Terrible business," he said and pressed his palms on the desk. "I haven't lost a student since becoming vice-principal, so I've had a few Zoom calls from advisors and trainers, explaining how best to deal with the media."

"You've been interviewed?"

"Of course. I was on *East Midlands Today* yesterday and I have an interview on BBC Radio Norfolk at lunchtime." It sounded like he was enjoying the attention. "I haven't had any dealings with the police, though."

"Is there any reason why you should have?"

He put his elbows on the desk and made a pyramid with his fingers. "Not at all. So did the police officer want to speak to you about Tuesday?"

I nodded.

"I see." He cleared his throat. "I understand you haven't been feeling too well."

Where had he heard that? "I feel fine."

"It must be unsettling for you, especially after the altercation on campus."

"I explained that, George."

"So you did." He regarded me gravely. "And yet, here we are, with the police on site speaking to a lecturer who had a disagreement on campus with a student who passed away."

It felt like he was trying to say something without being blunt. "And that's an issue?"

He wouldn't meet my gaze. "How could it not be, Kim? We all need to be on top of things at the moment."

"I understand that."

He bit his lip and shook his head as if I'd failed a basic test. "I was hoping I wasn't going to have to make this explicit, Kim."

"Explicit?"

"It's been reported that you've not been" – he shook his head again, more with pity this time – "feeling well. I won't press, but I assume it's a build-up of stress over what happened at the meeting and, subsequently, with Freddy."

Who'd told him this? Had Adam said something about my drinking last night? "What do you mean?"

George's colour faded a little. "I can't elaborate since it was passed to me in confidence."

"What's going on?"

Standing abruptly, he turned to look out the window. "I think it would be in the best interests of you and the college to take a few days away."

"I don't need to."

"It's not a request." He sighed. "Look at this from my point of view, Kim. Whether you admit it or not, there was clearly an issue between you and Freddy and it worries me you're not presenting an ideal professional front."

My temper rose. "Are you saying I'm being unprofessional?"

"No," he said too quickly and faced me. "I checked with HR and they agree the best course of action is for you to take a paid week off and get yourself together."

"I don't need to get myself together," I said, struggling to keep the anger out of my voice in case he thought I was being unprofessional. It was a fine line, one that I was frightened of slipping off. "I've always given you and the college my full attention and taught to the best of my ability. You must have agreed with that because you said as much when you told me to put in for the head of department."

He blanched and suddenly I knew why Adam had raised his eyebrows and rushed away. He wasn't heading to a class; he just didn't want to face me. I felt myself deflate. "Was there something else you wanted to tell me?"

"Not in this way, but yes. Of the two candidates for the role, you were the lead contender before this week. But the role has responsibilities beyond student welfare, Kim, and I can't have a head of department who's interviewed on campus by police or seen arguing with a student who later dies."

I felt empty. "I didn't ask for those things to happen, George. You know that and so does anyone else you'd be willing to ask. Hell, even bloody Ofsted would know that."

"That's enough," he said sharply. "I've made my decision and had it ratified by the governors. There's nothing to stop you going for the role in the future but, if you kick up a stink now, that can't help."

I bit my lip because he was right. His argument, however one-sided, was valid and if my blackmailer carried out their threat and released the CCTV pictures, then I'd be in even more trouble. I was stuck.

"I think we're done here, Kim." He sat down and took a file from his in-tray. "I'll get Pam to draft an email and have that sent through to you before the end of the day."

I knew he wanted me to walk away but I could see how uncomfortable he was and didn't want to dance completely to his tune. After a few moments, he looked up at me.

"Is there anything else?" He tried not to sound nervous but didn't quite succeed.

"No," I said and gave him a smile. "I'll take my week and get myself together, as you instructed. Then, hopefully, I'll be back in my position before the Ofsted inspection." I got up and walked out.

"Everything okay in there?" Pam asked.

"Not really," I said. "I'll see you in a week."

"In a week?" She sounded surprised.

"You'll be getting an email. I'll see you later."

I left the offices and leaned on the banister at the top of the stairs, breathing in through my nose and out through my mouth, trying to calm myself.

Was it Adam who'd said I was unwell, or did I let it slip somehow? I'd been drinking heavily this week, so it wasn't out of the question someone had smelt alcohol on me. I was in such a mess but knew I shouldn't accuse my friend of something I wasn't sure of, when I should have been congratulating him.

I rang him but it went to voicemail. I checked my watch.

"Idiot," I muttered. He was obviously in a lecture. "I just heard the news, Adam," I said to his voicemail. "Congratulations on the new role. I'll see you soon and hopefully we can celebrate. I also need to tell you my news. Take care."

Chapter 26

I sat at my desk with my head in my hands, annoyed at myself for feeling frustrated over a week's paid leave when Freddy's friends and family were grieving him.

When had I become so selfish?

I refreshed my email and one popped up from Pam. I opened it to find George officially advising me that my leave started with immediate effect.

"Nice one, George," I said then realised that was selfish, too. He might have been weak and reactive, but he was trying to protect the students, college and my colleagues, as well as himself. I didn't know if my mood was caused by still having alcohol in my system, or because I'd spent four days feeling sorry for myself, but I had to change my attitude otherwise I'd sink into a swamp of self-pity it would take me ages to crawl out of.

I needed to shake myself up and the only way to do that was talk everything through with Pops. He was level-headed and would absolutely tell me straight what he thought.

Feeling better for having made the decision, I put up an out-of-office notification and switched off the laptop.

I stopped by Adam's office, meaning to congratulate him, but his door was locked. The schedule posted on it read he was between classes, and I wondered where he was. Could he have gone out to celebrate? Why would he do that and not ask me? I felt a physical ache at the imagined slight, which was ridiculous. He knew I only wanted the best for him. Didn't he?

I shook my head to try and shift that thought process before it could gain traction. There wasn't an issue between us and I shouldn't waste my energy trying to manufacture one.

* * *

"Hello, love," Maureen said when I picked up the phone. She sounded worried. "I've got a bit of a problem, and I don't know how to deal with it."

"Can I help?"

"I don't know because it's about you. I got a letter hand-delivered this morning."

I stopped and leaned against a wall. Why would my blackmailer make their move now? I hadn't said anything to anyone. "Go on."

She exhaled audibly. "The envelope only had my name on and the note inside said 'you might be interested in something your so-called friend Kim did' and there was a folded piece of paper. I opened it enough to see it was a poor-quality picture with writing and numbers on it, like you see when people get speeding fines. I saw your head and the young man who was attacked on the beach."

"Were we outside in the dark?"

"It looked that way. It's very poor quality. Is it from the garage, love?"

"I think so, it's like the one I got delivered." My phone beeped to let me know I had another call. I ignored it.

"I thought you'd like to know."

"I do and I appreciate it, Maureen. You did the right thing."

"Are you going to tell the police?"

"I need to do something," I said, to mollify her.

"Good, don't let the bastards grind you down."

"I won't."

"And good luck for tonight. I'll see you there and I hope you give Glover hell."

"Oh, I will."

We said our goodbyes.

As unpleasant as it was to know Maureen had been pulled into the orbit of my nightmare, at least I knew the blackmail had to be centred around the golf course proposal. It was little consolation, but it gave me a focus. So this person wanted me to keep my mouth shut and Freddy was the stick they were using to threaten my career if I didn't. Had he been trying to confess when he met me at the refectory?

"Fuck me," I muttered. I had to find a hole in this train of thought because if I didn't, it meant I'd uncovered some kind of conspiracy and that felt ridiculous. Why would anyone go to this amount of fuss and bother to get a local councillor to change her vote? And, worse, did it mean Freddy was attacked because he was trying to warn me?

Chapter 27

The caller I'd missed left a voicemail message.

"Hi, this is for Kim Morgan. My name is Trevor Evans and I'm a journalist with the *Seagrave Telegraph*. I wanted to speak to you about the unfortunate death of Freddy Medwin because, as I understand it, you're a lecturer at the college where he was a student. If you could ring me back, that would be excellent, or else I'll ring you in an hour or so. Thanks for your time."

I'd never heard of Trevor Evans and deleted his message. I doubted his interest in me was due to my being a lecturer, when it was more likely he'd heard about the incident at the refectory. I had absolutely no interest in speaking to any journalists, local or otherwise.

I turned into Market Street, where several pavement cafes were doing a good trade as patrons sat at little bistro tables enjoying the Indian summer and sipping tea and coffee.

Halfway along the street, I happened to look up and saw a blue Mini crossed the junction at the end of the road. In panic, I ducked behind a spinner rack filled with postcards, outside a newsagent's. The car didn't slow down, and I couldn't tell if it was Ogilvy but, within a handful of seconds, it was out of sight.

Annoyed the car had generated such a reaction, I kept watching the junction as I walked. I started to cross the road and glanced behind me to make sure there was no traffic coming. The blue Mini turned into Market Street and my breath caught in my throat when I saw the number plate was HK72.

"Shit." I rushed across the road. How could he have found me?

I reached the kerb and the car was close enough I could see Ogilvy. He waved jauntily, like we were old friends. I didn't wave back and walked away briskly. There weren't any cafes at this end, and I debated turning around and heading back to them, but then he could cut me off and I didn't want that. I had no idea what he planned to do but I didn't want to make it easier for him to approach me.

The end of the road was a couple of hundred yards away and I wasn't walking fast enough to outpace him.

Tyres squealed against a kerbstone and a door slammed. I glanced over my shoulder, and he was about twenty feet behind me and crossing the road. He wore a dark suit and looked like he'd just come out of an important meeting.

"Hey, Kim," he called. "Hold up there, love."

I picked up my pace until I was almost jogging, looking for a quick escape. There was a flatbed works van at the kerb ahead of me. Across the road was the large Victorian building now used as an indoor market. An A-frame sign outside announced it was hosting a flea market today. If I could get into there, I might be able to lose him.

Just before I reached the van, I looked over my shoulder. Ogilvy had obviously had the same thought and, rather than follow me onto the pavement, was tracking along the road. If I dodged across, he could easily catch me.

Further on, I could see an alley between two shops on my right.

If I pretended to duck around the front of the van, he might move to cut me off and then I could dart down the alley while the van hid me from his view. It was a long shot, but I didn't have too many other options.

"Don't be silly, Kim," he called. "You can't run away from me forever."

I ducked down when I reached the van and ran past it in a half-crouch, trying to keep out of sight.

Gravel crunched under his brogues, and I heard him slide. "Shit!"

Adrenalin drove me on, and I ran as quickly as I could, knowing I didn't have a lot of time before he figured out what I was doing. I ducked into the alley.

It sloped down and was made gloomy by the high walls on either side. Nobody was coming towards me and I ran. Halfway down, where a pile of rubbish had been stacked haphazardly by a propped open door with 'Keep Closed' written on, was a small flight of concrete steps that led me onto another narrow alley. There was more rubbish here and, judging by the smell, most of it was from a food place. I kept going, checking behind me every now and again but he wasn't following me.

The alley finished at Marine Drive and as I stepped in the sunshine my hands were jittery, like ants were crawling under the skin. I wanted to stop and take a breath but didn't dare, in case Ogilvy came after me. I made fists and stretched out my fingers until the jitters had gone and walked briskly for five minutes.

When I was sure he wasn't anywhere near me, I got a coffee from a little takeaway booth and walked to Pops' building.

Chapter 28

Pops let me in when I buzzed and met me on the landing. "What's the matter, treacle?"

"Not much." It didn't seem to placate him. "It's been a bit of a day."

"It must be, if you aren't at work." He took my elbow gently and we went into his flat. He was barefoot, wearing denim cut-offs and an undone short-sleeved shirt. His hair was immaculate. "Head out to the balcony and I'll make us a drink. Something cold or a cuppa?"

"A glass of water would be lovely." I felt some of my stress lift. I was safe now, indoors and with Pops.

He went into the kitchen, and I went through to the balcony. I sat on the chair in the shade and slipped my shoes off. I put my bare feet into the sun and wiggled my toes. It felt nice. A camera on a tripod pointed out over the water and the attached telephoto lens looked old but well-maintained and was supported by a pole.

Pops came out and put a tray on the table. He handed me a pint glass stocked with ice cubes and sat on a chair across from me in the full glare of the sun. He'd made himself a coffee and it smelled lovely.

"Cheers," he said and gave me a little smile. "So, what's happening? Did you want to talk about it?"

"If you don't mind." I gestured to the camera. "I don't want to interrupt your work."

He made a 'pah' sound and waved his hand towards the horizon. "Nothing's more important than you and I can take pictures of boats at any time. You go ahead."

"I don't know where to start," I said honestly.

"At the beginning, treacle. Always start at the beginning."

I told him everything, right up to my talk with DS Richards this morning and was discreet about the garage incident but he still raised his eyebrows slightly. He didn't speak but listened attentively, giving me his full attention as he sipped his coffee.

"Blimey, my girl. You've got yourself into a bit of a pickle here, haven't you?" He put his now empty cup on the floor by the leg of his chair. "But how do you feel in yourself? I mean, it must have been a shock. How are you dealing with this Freddy lad passing away?"

"I'm sad he died, obviously, but I'm not grieving. The fact I crossed a professional line weighs on me and so does the thought I could lose my job if work found out about it."

He nodded. "Were you intending to get frisky when you went to the garage?"

"Not at all."

"In which case it wasn't premeditated, so you didn't cross a line. And what would work do?"

"I broke the number one rule, Pops. I had a relationship with a student."

"I perfectly understand your anxiety, but the argument you didn't know has to weigh in your favour. And if it doesn't, he was in his twenties and you're just out of yours, you're both adults and it was consensual. Semantics aside, what did you do wrong?"

"You're right, I know you are but…"

"But nothing, treacle. I came of age in the sixties and even though it took a while for the free-love movement to hit East Anglia, I've been in situations where the hormones take over and you're pretty much hostage to them."

"You have no idea how much it means to hear that, Pops." And it did. His moral centre was rock solid and he would never lie to me.

"For what it's worth, though, you should have told the police everything at the start."

"I know, but…"

"But it's difficult, I get that." He tapped his lips with his finger, which he often did when he was thinking. "And you thought he was sending you the notes?"

"I did."

"Presumably because he's a poor student who thought you might want to pay to keep your indiscretion from being displayed to the world?"

"Something like that."

"But it's clearly not him, which leaves you with Caitlin and this Ogilvy fella, who I'd very much like to have a word with. She doesn't sound very pleasant, either, but can you see her sending those notes?"

"I wouldn't have said so before, but my perception of her has changed this week." I blew out my breath. "I don't know who to trust."

"What about Adam? What's his take on the situation?"

"We haven't discussed it."

Pops shook his head slightly. "You're right, it's odd but everything seems to come from the protest meeting." He tapped his lip again. "I've had a thought, but it might come from reading too many Mike Hammer novels."

I sat forward, elbows on my knees. "I'm willing to listen to any theory you have."

"Let's ignore, for the moment, the fact that with Glover's array of contacts, he'll get his own way in the end, whatever happens. Instead, think about the link between him and Freddy."

My headache was creeping back. "I don't know what the link is."

"What if they're blackmailing you because they knew you and Freddy were going to happen."

"I did think of that."

"You're clearly reading the classics," he said and reached for his coffee. He looked disappointed it was all gone. "Freddy might not have been in on the honeypot trap itself, just a component part of it. That would explain what he meant about you not knowing the truth and also why he was surprised you were a lecturer."

"He might have been acting."

"What if he wasn't, though? What if someone pointed him in your direction knowing there might be a spark?"

"But what could anyone get from doing that to me? Especially when the fallout to both me and Freddy could be huge."

We looked at one another and shrugged at the same time.

"What if his attack was linked to the fact he tried to tell you the truth?"

I shivered at the implication. "I hadn't thought of that."

"Perhaps I'm wrong but, as Sherlock says in *The Sign of Four*, when you eliminate the impossible, whatever remains, however improbable, must be the truth." He smiled. "I may have paraphrased that."

"It sounds as sensible as anything else."

"Too sensible," he said and shook his head. "It feels like we took a misstep somewhere."

"I thought the same thing. It's like I'm missing a jigsaw piece but can't put my finger on it."

"Is it worth looking at Ryan's pictures again with fresh eyes? If everything started at the meeting, then you might see a photograph of Freddy talking to Ogilvy or Caitlin. If you found something like that, we could work our way backwards."

"That's not a bad idea," I mused. And it was better than standing still and waiting for Ogilvy to catch up with me.

"I'm full of them," he said. "But if you think I'm smart, let me tell you what happened when I used Ryan's camera."

"Did you break it?"

"No, but I got the setting wrong and took a photograph every minute for eight hours." He laughed. "It went all through the night. Can you believe it?"

I felt a jolt of nervous excitement. "You filmed all night on Tuesday looking towards the pier?"

"I did." He laughed. "It took ages to watch it through."

"Do you still have it?"

"Yes. Ryan downloaded it to my tablet."

My excitement grew. "Can I see it?"

"If you're sure you want to. It's really not that exciting."

"It might not be, but I think I'm having my own Mike Spanner moment."

"It's Mike Hammer," he corrected me.

"He was well before my time, Pops."

"Cheeky little bugger," he said and went into the lounge. He came back wearing glasses and carrying his tablet, which he put on the table. He quickly found the file. "Did you want to see all of it?"

"Not, just the stuff from late evening into early morning."

He made the connection himself then and I heard the excitement in his voice. "Right! Of course. Do you think I caught Freddy's attackers on film?"

"We can't see the beach, but we might see people on the street."

"Good thinking. This feels like when we had a breaking story on the *Telegraph*."

"If you caught something, then you're part of that breaking story, Pops."

He moved the time bar on the video and pressed play. "I've set it to show each still for a second, so we should see something. If it ran at normal speed, at best we'd just see a blur."

The image was crisp and clear, if a little yellow. The lower edge of the pier was at the top of the frame and I could see a good portion of Marine Drive and the pavement on the waterside.

We watched for a couple of minutes and then a car was at the kerb. "Stop!" I said.

Pops paused the image and I pointed at the vehicle. My stomach fluttered.

"Does that look like a Mini to you?"

"It could be," he said.

"Can you make the colour any clearer?"

"Not really. The spectrum is thrown by the streetlight, but I'd say it was either blue or green." He looked at me curiously. "Do you know that car?"

"I'm not sure, but Ogilvy drives a blue Mini."

"I'll go back a few frames to see when it turned up."

"Good thinking, Mike Hammer."

He flashed me a quick smile and wound the video back until the car wasn't there. "Eleven forty-two," he said.

Pops moved the frames on. There were a couple of blurs as cars drove by, but the pavement remained clear. Then someone was in the middle of the frame, wearing pale clothes and walking alone.

"Eleven fifty-six," he said. "Wouldn't it be weird if we'd caught Freddy on film?"

Two more frames and then someone was on the pavement beside the Mini, turned away from the car so it was impossible to see their face. They wore darker clothes.

"Who's that?" I asked. "Do you suppose they got out of the car?"

"They might have, or it could be a pedestrian talking to whoever is in the car."

The person wasn't in the next frame or the next and Pops moved on briskly. He stopped when the time stamp had moved by twenty-four minutes and nothing had changed in that time.

"Perhaps the person lives nearby and parks there." He sounded disappointed.

"Could be." I was disappointed, too, because I wanted that to be Ogilvy's Mini and I wanted to see him walk towards the pier.

Pops moved on and the time stamp read a little after one, when someone appeared on the pavement coming from the direction of the beach.

We exchanged a glance and he moved on a frame. The person was next to the Mini. They weren't in the next and the car had gone by the fourth.

It felt like we'd just witnessed the aftermath of something. "If the person walked towards the pier, then why did he or she come back to the car from the direction of the beach?"

"It's unlikely they'd be hanging around the pier, even if they were trying to pick someone up," Pops said. "The pier is filled with CCTV because of the theatre, so most of the junkies and whoever else head down to the old lido."

"Whoever it was, they were on the beach around the time Freddy got attacked. Or did it themselves."

"That's a nasty idea."

"I know." It made me feel a little queasy. "What if the person in lighter clothes is Freddy and the driver is the attacker? That means it's not random."

"I'm sure the police would have checked the CCTV on Marine Drive."

"But would they look at a car that was there long before the victim? What if the driver knew Freddy was going to walk by at a certain time and lay in wait? It would look perfectly innocent to any outsiders and more so if the attacker came back from a different angle."

"You could have a point there. If they were interviewed, they could say they were watching the sea for a while." He clapped his hands once. "We need to show this to the police. They'll be able to cross-reference the car with other CCTV footage and get the number plate."

I edged my chair into the sunlight. It was frightening to think I might have been interacting with Freddy's killer without realising, but I still couldn't figure out why Ogilvy set a honeytrap for me in the first place. My mind turned somersaults trying to make a connection. "I think I should check Ryan's photographs again. Something in them might back up your footage."

"We don't have a lot of time, though. You're voting tonight, so Ogilvy's got to make his move soon."

"What if you took the video footage to DS Richards and I go to see Ryan?"

"Split up? Are you quite mad, young lady?"

"I'll be careful."

"And Ogilvy could be anywhere waiting for you. I can't let you go on your own."

"I'm not ten, Pops."

"No, that's a fact." He smiled ruefully then clicked his fingers. "I know! Why don't you take Betty? A crash helmet won't be much of a disguise but if Ogilvy is watching for you, he won't suspect a woman on a Vespa."

"That's a great idea." Except I hadn't ridden the scooter in a long time.

"Like I said, I'm full of them."

We went into the hall. There was a side table by the door and he handed me a set of keys from a dish on top. He took a white crash helmet from underneath and handed it to me. We put our shoes on, left the floor and walked down to the ground floor. His knee started to make a horrible popping sound after the first flight.

"Are you going to be okay walking to the police station?" I asked with concern.

"I'm not ten, treacle, I can manage. And if I can't, I'll flag down a taxi."

A narrow corridor opened off the foyer and we walked down it to a small utility room that led out to the back garden. There was a small patio with four sheds on it. He unlocked the nearest one and there was Betty, on her kickstand, gleaming in all her glory.

I helped him get the Vespa out of the shed and wheeled the bike to the back gate. He opened it and leaned out to look both ways along the street before giving me the thumbs up. I put the helmet on then pushed the scooter to the road.

"Be careful," he said. "I don't want you coming off and hurting yourself."

"I'll be fine. You take it easy, too."

"What time's the meeting?"

"It starts at seven."

"I'll be there." He tapped twice lightly on top of the helmet.

I switched the engine on and put the bike into gear. "Thank you," I said and lurched away from the kerb. I got a quick glimpse of his worried face but by the time I was halfway down the street, I'd remembered how to ride.

Chapter 29

Although I was sure no one had followed me, I only took my helmet off once I was inside the tourist information office. As I ran my fingers through my hair, Ryan came through from the back office.

"Hello," he said, obviously surprised. "I was expecting your granddad when I heard the Vespa."

"Yeah, sorry about that. Can I come through?"

"Sure." He lifted the counter flap. "Did you want a cuppa?"

"A coffee I could stand a spoon up in."

"I can do that."

We went into the back office and I leaned against the table while he went into the kitchen. "Am I interrupting you?"

"Only from archiving but since you're the third person who's come in today, I'm not exactly run off my feet."

He came through and handed me a mug. "It's none of my business and tell me to shut up if you want, but is there a reason why you're here in the early afternoon of a school day?"

"Kind of." I told him what had happened so far this morning and his eyebrows steadily crept up in surprise. "So, with Pops' footage, we think Ogilvy might have had something to do with Freddy being attacked."

"He told me the footage wasn't very successful."

"It wasn't, for what he wanted, but he filmed towards the pier."

"He filmed the attack?"

"No, but the pier is at the top of the frame. We used the timeline and I'm sure it shows Freddy walking along the pavement and being followed by someone who gets out of a car. There's not enough detail to see who it is, but Ogilvy drives a Mini and that's what we think the car is."

"You need to take that to the police."

"Pops is doing that now. I came here because I wanted to run through your photographs of the event again, to see if we can link them together."

The bell over the door jangled and we looked at each other in surprise. "Customer number four," he said. "I'll be back in a minute."

"Of course."

He went into the outer office and began talking with the person who'd come in. My phone rang a few moments later and Adam's smiling face filled the screen.

"Hi," I said. "I tried to find you before, to say congratulations, but you weren't about."

"Hello and thank you. I got your message and appreciated it. I'm well chuffed, as you can imagine, though I still think you were the better candidate. What was your news?"

"Didn't you hear? George sent me home for a week. I got another visit from DS Richards, and he wasn't happy about it."

"He can't do that." Adam was indignant. "I'll get the union onto it."

"No, because you don't want to piss him off straight away. Let him have his power play then I'll go back and be guided by you."

"You're taking this very well, Kim. I'm not sure how gracious I'd be if I hadn't got the job." He laughed, as if to make me aware he was joking but there was a tinge of embarrassment to it. "So where are you now? Are you at home?"

"No, I'm out and about. I had another a run-in with that Ogilvy bloke. He chased me and I went to Pops' place."

"Bloody hell, that's awful. Did you report it?"

"No, because we got distracted. Pops filmed the pier on the night Freddy Medwin was attacked."

"Did he catch the attack?" he asked, incredulous.

"No, but you can see a man in the area at the time of it. Pops has taken the footage to the police, all the same. I'm just going through the photographs of the event with Ryan, to see if I can see something to tie Ogilvy in with Freddy."

"Bloody hell," he said. "And it's the vote tonight, isn't it? Did you want me to pick you up in case he tries anything else?"

"No, but thank you. I'll see you there."

The bell tinkled and Ryan came back into the office. "Sorry about that," he said.

"Don't be silly, I'm interrupting your working day. I should leave."

"But this," he said and pointed at me and then his own chest, "is working. This is an information office and I'm happy to be helping the granddaughter of a wonderful friend of mine."

Ryan pulled a chair towards the desk and we sat down together, side by side. He angled the laptop so we could both see the screen.

"How about I run through all the photographs first and see if anything leaps out at you? We can then use the facial ID software again." He opened the first image. "Say stop if you need to."

We moved through the pictures slowly.

"Wait," I said. "Go back one."

He did and the photograph showed me ushering Maureen off stage towards Adam, who held her arm. Freddy was right behind him, close enough that Adam must have been aware of him. I got an odd feeling, as if there was something in the image I wasn't quite seeing.

Ryan looked at me. "Are you looking at something specific?"

"No, we can move on."

He did and it wasn't long before we finished the run. "That's pretty much it and nothing seemed out of place to me."

"Or me," I said with mounting frustration. "Other than I was surprised to see Freddy and Adam being so close together."

"Okay, we'll try it now with the facial recognition on. Do you want me to run it on Ogilvy or Freddy?"

"Go for Ogilvy first."

Ryan opened the first image, where Ogilvy was standing behind me, and pressed a button. He moved the square that appeared so it covered Ogilvy's face. He pressed another button and half a dozen smaller images appeared down the side of the screen.

"That's more than I thought I saw," I said.

We reviewed them steadily and he was lurking in the background of most. The last photograph was of a few people talking in the shadows on the balcony.

"Is that really Ogilvy?"

"Patience," said Ryan. His fingers moved swiftly over the keyboard and the image got lighter as the shadows seemed to recede. "Do you recognise her?"

"Oh shit," I said.

Chapter 30

Ogilvy was standing with Caitlin and facing a third person turned away from the camera enough that I couldn't tell if they were male or female. Caitlin was scowling and Ogilvy was talking with his hands raised as if he was making a point.

It felt like a band was tightening over my chest. "She told me she wasn't there."

"Who is it?"

"That's Caitlin Alexander. She's the one who asked you for the photographs."

"Why would she lie to you? And why ask me?"

Perfect questions to ask and I had no idea what the perfect answers were. Why would she lie? It felt like I'd lost another couple of pieces from the jigsaw puzzle. What was the link between her and Ogilvy? My mind took a dark turn. What if the thugs had been organised by Ogilvy and Caitlin? She might have been there, hidden away in the shadows, to make sure everything went to plan.

How had I managed to read her so wrong? I thought I was a pretty good judge of character, but I'd clearly been way off the mark.

Another darker thought hit me then.

If Ogilvy did have something to do with Freddy's attack, did she know about it?

"I don't understand any of this," I said. What had we stumbled over here?

"It could be something simple," Ryan said. "Perhaps they went to school together or they're neighbours and were catching up. It could be anything."

"No, they're not the same age and she lives in a big place on Radnor Road."

"Perhaps there's another shared interest then?"

"She's an early-bird investor of the golf course and he's been trying to speak to me about it."

"Would that be enough for her to take a risk and try to discredit you and the protest?"

"It all depends on how much money she'd stand to make." It would be all too easy to fall into some kind of conspiracy theory rabbit hole with this, but it felt like we'd made a discovery here. "This could be the reason why the protest meeting seems to be the catalyst for all the weird and horrible things that have happened this week."

"It'd have to be a lot of money, though, surely?"

"Who knows? I assumed she was well off, but some people never have enough, do they?" My frustration was growing. "If she is involved, then there's no point, is there? Maybe it'd be better if I missed the vote."

"Are you serious?"

"Why not? It doesn't matter, in the grand scheme of things, as there's already been a lot of hassle for potentially nothing. Not to mention that Freddy's death might, perhaps, be linked to Ogilvy."

"I see what you're saying, but it doesn't mean everything's linked. There's plenty of hassle, I'll give you that, but are you making connections where none exist? You're assuming Caitlin doesn't know Ogilvy socially. For all you know, she could have been there to sound out the support for the protest and just didn't want you to think she was checking up on you."

His theory made a lot more sense than my ravings. "You think I'm being silly?"

"No. I think you're caught in the middle of something that, even to me, looks odd and you can't quite see the wood for the trees. I also think you feel guilty about Freddy."

"So I'm being paranoid?"

"I didn't say that. But perhaps you're looking at things that aren't as cut and dried as you think they are."

That, at least, made sense. "So maybe I just need to walk away from it all."

"Why would you do that? The people of Seagrave want someone – no, they deserve someone – who's going to fight for them. That's what you're doing and there's a lot of strength in that."

"To what end? Glover will steamroller me; the proposal will be passed and Caitlin will make her money."

"But if the vote goes against him, it'll slow the process and then maybe something else will get in the way. If you back out now, he wins, and the marshlands disappear under concrete." He laughed sourly at himself. "Listen to me, spouting like a twat. I'm trying to charge you up and I never volunteered to help with the council."

His deprecation forced a chuckle out of me and that seemed to break the tension, though our laughter had a slightly hysteric feel to it. Even so, it helped fracture my negative energy. He was right, I could see that and the only thing I could control was my ability to throw a spanner in the works. Perhaps that would be enough for people to be able to see what was going on.

"You're right," I said when I calmed down. "I'll go and vote and try to keep out of Caitlin and Ogilvy's way."

"Why don't I come with you? If Ogilvy is in that footage, then it proves he's dangerous."

As much as him escorting me sounded comforting, I wanted to do this on my own to prove I could. Plus, I had to go home and shower. "Thanks, but no. He won't recognise me in the crash helmet and if he's outside my building, I'll ride on by."

"If you're sure," he said, dubiously. "I'll go back through the photographs and see if I can find anything else, then meet you at the college."

"The meeting's at seven." I stood up. "Don't be late."

Chapter 31

It was almost four when I got home. I walked Betty around the side of the building and chained her to the back fence in the communal garden area. I didn't take the helmet off until I'd let myself into the front door just in case Ogilvy was keeping an eye out for me.

I checked my phone as I walked up the stairs. I'd missed a call as I was riding home and it was the same number as before.

"Hi, this is Trevor Evans from the *Seagrave Telegraph* and I'd like to speak to Kim Morgan. I rang earlier and was hoping to catch you before the public vote later. Basically, I'd like to talk to you about the untimely death of Freddy Medwin and your links to him. If you could ring me back, I'd very much appreciate it, but I will try again. Thank you."

I wanted to smash the message off the phone and was tempted to punch the screen but contented myself with making a strangled scream before I pressed delete. I didn't know what he was going to ask, but I doubted it'd be something I'd dignify with an answer. I certainly wouldn't be calling him back.

When I reached my floor, I could faintly hear music from my neighbour's flat. I opened the door, braced to find another note but nothing was on the mat. As soon as I closed the door, though, I knew something was wrong.

The flat felt different.

I've lived here on my own long enough to know the space almost intimately and something was a little off. It didn't feel like there was anyone in there with me but there was definitely the sensation someone had been. Goosebumps pebbled my arms and the little hairs on the back of my neck stood up.

I pressed my back to the door and looked down the hall. From what I could see, the kitchen and lounge both appeared to be empty. My bedroom door was two feet away and slightly ajar, as I always left it.

My first option was to leave and the second was to investigate. As much as I wanted to get out, I was thoroughly fed up with things going on that I had little control over and this was just another incident to add to the list. I'd had enough. The flat felt empty, but what if I was wrong? What if someone was hiding behind a door, just waiting for me to go by? I had to check.

I picked up a heeled shoe from the rack and edged forward. I held my breath but could only hear the faint beat of my neighbour's music. I toed the door open and rushed into the bedroom with the shoe and crash helmet raised, thinking I could hit the intruder with either weapon and put them down long enough to call the police.

The room was empty. I checked down by the side of the bed and in the wardrobe. The window was set to airlock and firmly fastened.

My heart was thumping and the blood rushed in my ears loud enough that I thought it might be audible to other people.

I edged out and slipped along the wall to the bathroom. The door was wide open. Sunlight streamed through the window and the shower curtain was pulled back. Nobody was behind the door.

I felt frustrated and a little silly – I was like a kid frightened by the bogeyman. Why was I letting someone do this to me? If anyone was in there, they'd already heard me so why give them the pleasure of seeing me scared?

I kicked the lounge door open, shoe and helmet raised. "Come on then, you bastard," I said and strode into the room. I checked behind the sofa, but nobody was in here. The French windows were locked. It was when I turned to go into the kitchen that I saw something wrong.

I'd been reading a Sue Grafton novel, and it was on the mouse mat to the right of my laptop. Except I hadn't left it there. I liked space when I worked and always put things on the left of the laptop, well away from my hand. The hairs on the back of my neck prickled to attention again.

I went into the kitchen a little more cautiously, but it was empty, too, and the fanlight window, which someone would have to as slim as a snake to fit through, was locked. There was a faint smell in the air, a slightly musky scent almost like aftershave.

The coffee mug I'd used this morning was in front of the kettle and I knew I'd put it into the dishwasher before I left, because that was part of my routine. I never left dirty cups or plates out. It was as if someone had deliberately put it there to let me know they'd invaded my space.

Now I was scared and felt a tightness in my chest and across my forehead. I leaned against the worktop and tried to calm myself by forcing my breathing into a steadier rhythm. It took a while before I felt okay.

How had the person got in? The front door had been locked and so were the windows.

My mobile rang, startling a shriek out of me and I didn't know what I'd do if it said 'number withheld'. It didn't. The call was from Ryan.

"Hi."

"Hi, Kim. What's up? You sound worried."

"I'm okay, but I think someone's been in the flat."

"You've been broken into? Bloody hell, have you called the police?"

Why hadn't I thought of that before? "No, I've only just got in here."

"Okay, but have they gone? Are you safe?"

"I am. The flat's empty."

"Good. Then call the police and don't sweep up the glass or try to tidy where they've made a mess."

"They didn't leave any mess."

"Nothing at all? Did you lock your door?"

"Of course I did."

"Oh." He was quiet for a few moments. "Did they take anything?"

"I don't think so." I went into the bedroom and opened the drawer where I kept my jewellery box. It hadn't been moved and, when I lifted the lid, everything was where it should have been. I checked another drawer, where I kept cash I'd saved, but it was all there. "No, they didn't take anything."

"If they didn't break a window or the lock and didn't take anything, how do you know anyone's been there?"

"Because things have been moved."

"Things have been…" he started but didn't finish. I knew, then, I wasn't going to ring the police.

"Stuff's out of place," I insisted, painfully aware of how weird that sounded. "They've put a book in the wrong place and my mug was on the worktop."

"A book and a mug?"

"I know how it must sound, but I'm right."

"I'm sure," he said and sounded like a man trying to make sense of something he didn't understand. "But how did they get in if everything was locked? Does anyone have a spare key?"

"Only Pops," I said.

"Nobody else?"

Adam gave me his back on the day we broke up. We'd been sitting on the beach and once he realised I wasn't going to change my mind, he took my key from his keyring and handed it to me like he was making a symbolic gesture. "No." If the roles were reversed, I wouldn't have believed me either. "I know I'm right," I insisted.

"I believe you."

"No, you don't, you think I'm going mad."

"I think you've been under a lot of stress and that can do odd things to the mind."

"So, I'm seeing things?"

"Not at all." He took a deep breath and exhaled slowly. "I'm sorry, Kim, I'm trying to be supportive, I really am. Did you want me to come over?"

"No, you're okay. I'll go mad on my own, thanks."

"You're not mad, Kim."

"Well, I'm something. So anyway, you rang me. What were you after?"

"Well, it's…" He tapered off, as if he wasn't sure about saying more. "I found another picture of your colleague, whose name I've forgotten. The one who helped Maureen."

"Adam?"

"Yes. I ran a check on Freddy, and he was in another photograph on the balcony, which I had to lighten. Him and Adam are standing side by side, deep in conversation."

"Was that before or after the one where Adam's near the stage?"

"After."

"But Adam told me he didn't know Freddy before the incident at the refectory."

"Maybe they just found themselves standing next to one another, after helping Maureen and fell into conversation."

"If that was the case, Adam would have recognised him on campus." I bit the inside of my cheek. "It doesn't make sense."

"There might be a perfectly rational explanation. You'll have to ask him if you see him at the meeting."

"I will."

"Are you sure you don't want me to come around?"

"I'm certain but thank you. I need to have a shower and a quick bite to eat before I head out."

"I'll see you at the meeting. Be careful."

I deadlocked the front door and put on the security chain before I got undressed for my shower. I locked the bathroom door, too, just in case.

Chapter 32

Nobody tried to get into the bathroom and, after I'd dried myself, I held my breath and went into the hall. It was empty. I exhaled shakily.

My hands were clammy with nerves, but I also felt like I'd overreacted and hated that someone was making me feel like this. I should be angry at their violation of my space, not a cowering wreck scared of walking around the place I should feel safest in.

Pulling my shoulders back, I stood up straight. "I'm not going to be frightened," I said. It didn't feel as good saying it out loud as I'd hoped it would.

I got dressed, made a coffee and some cheese on toast and went through the messenger bag I use for council business. Everything seemed to be in there. I checked my phone but there were no messages from Pops. I made a point of putting my mug and plate in the dishwasher then let myself out the flat, locking the door securely.

The landing was clear and next door's music competed with my thumping heart.

"Come on," I said, trying to motivate myself.

I went downstairs and, in an effort to not think someone was waiting to grab me at every landing, I thought about Ryan's call. What he'd told me still didn't make sense. Why would Adam lie about knowing Freddy? A lie, in my experience, was never as important as the reason it was told in the first place, so what did Adam gain by telling me he didn't know Freddy?

There was one way to find out.

I rang him and it went straight to voicemail. I checked my watch and saw it was a little after six. He might have still been at work if he was doing some revision courses, or George had asked to discuss his head of department ideas. I wondered idly if he was going to lift any of the ones I'd mentioned to him.

"Hi, it's Kim. I hoped to have a quick word before the meeting, but I'll speak to you afterwards. See you."

I reached the foyer without incident and looked out onto Marlborough Street. As far as I could tell, there weren't any blue Minis at the kerb. I put my hand on the door handle and stopped. Just because I couldn't see his car didn't mean Ogilvy wasn't out of sight and waiting for me.

I don't know if it was due to paranoia or terror, but there didn't seem to be much point in deliberately putting myself in harm's way. I hadn't planned to take Betty because, if he was watching me, the crash helmet wasn't a disguise and once I was on the scooter, it wouldn't be hard to drive into me.

The mailboxes for the flats were on the wall to my left and there was a table underneath them, where the postman put bulky packages. It was also a holding area for the menus, freebies and junk mail that came every day. Someone had made piles of items and there were three small stacks of cards for taxis, Ubers and private hire limos. I picked up the first one on the taxi pile and rang the number. The controller said they had a car just finishing a job a couple of streets over and I booked it.

"I'll wait for him in the foyer," I said.

"No worries. Give him five minutes. His name's Guy."

"Thanks," I said and went to wait by the door.

The taxi arrived in less than five minutes and the driver waved at me through the passenger window. I rushed down the steps and across the pavement.

"Alright, love?" he asked as I got in. "I'm Guy." Somewhere in his late fifties, he had a boxing-flattened nose and a small trilby was perched on his thinning hair. "Where are we heading?"

"The Town Campus of Seagrave College."

"No problem." He looked at me intently for a moment. "Have I seen you around before?"

"I don't think so, but I've been in the paper. I'm Kim Morgan and I'm on the council."

He clicked his fingers. "That's the ticket! You're opposing that golf course, aren't you?"

"I am," I said and hoped he shared my viewpoint.

"Good for you, girl. It's nice to see the council standing up to people with money who think they can get away with anything. Is it the vote tonight?"

"Uh-huh. That's where I'm going."

"I'm pleased to be taking you," he said and drove off at pace.

I scanned both sides of Marlborough Street as best I could but didn't see any sign of Ogilvy or his Mini. I checked in the side mirror and nothing seemed to be following us. I took out my phone and rang Pops.

"I was just about to ring you, treacle."

"How did it go?"

"Grand, other than worrying about you. I've literally just this minute got back from the station. Your lady was there and we went into a back office to talk. I told her about you and what we saw and then showed her the footage."

"What did she think?"

"She didn't say much, but they're trained to be cagey, aren't they? She wanted a copy, so I let her keep the tablet and they're going to download the footage then give it back to me. She said she'd be in touch."

"At least she took it seriously."

"How could she not?" he asked flatly. "Even if the person in the car didn't do anything, they might have seen something that could help with the investigation." He paused a moment. "Are you in a car?"

"I'm in a taxi, heading for the college."

"You didn't take Betty?"

"No, I thought it safer to leave her at my place."

"Okay," he said, and I heard the catch in his voice. He knew I liked walking, so if I wasn't on foot or riding Betty then something must be wrong.

"Don't worry," I said, before he had a chance to ask. "There's some details I need to go over and I can read while I ride."

"If you're sure," he said but didn't sound convinced. "I'll see you later. I'm looking forward to seeing you get one over on Brian Glover."

Chapter 33

Guy dropped me at the campus car park entrance. A police car was a little further along the road with an officer leaning against the wing as she looked at her phone.

"My number's on here," Guy said and handed me a card. "If you ever need taking anywhere or a quick getaway, give me a holler."

"Thanks." I took my credit card out, but he waved it away.

"Nah. Tell Brian Glover what's what and that's payment for me."

"You're a gent," I said and got out.

"Probably not." He grinned. "Give them hell, love."

He drove away and I took my college and council lanyards out of my bag and put them on. The police officer glanced at me and put her phone in one of the pockets on her stab vest.

"You don't usually see the police at council meetings."

"I know," she said and glanced at my lanyards. "You're on the council?"

"I'm Kim Morgan."

"Ah, you're the one who was at the meeting where everything kicked off."

"That's right. Are you expecting trouble again?"

"Hopefully not, we're basically here to make sure there's no ruckus." She jerked her chin towards the car park. "The protest group are allowed on the grounds but not inside. My colleague is making sure they comply, but they seem like a good bunch."

"They are."

"I'm sure. Have a safe meeting, Councillor Morgan."

I followed the footpath around to the car park. There weren't many cars and I saw Adam's in its usual spot. The protest group, some of them with placards, were gathered over a handful of spaces. Others were sitting on deckchairs, including Maureen who was chatting to the secretary. A couple behind her were trying to unfurl a banner.

One of the men saw me and called "Hello!" and the others joined in. People seemed pleased to see me and I was happy to see them. I spoke to a few as I walked over to Maureen. She tried to stand up but her knee wasn't bending.

"Stay sitting," I said.

"I absolutely will not." There was a determined set to her jaw and it took her a moment, but she got to her feet. "If they'd put bionic knees like this into Steve Austin, that series wouldn't have lasted half as long." I could see the pain behind her smile. "It's good to see you, Kim."

"And you. I hope you're not planning to get into any trouble tonight?"

"I'll try my hardest not to, but I can't promise." She smiled. "Apparently, I'm allowed in, but the others have to stay out here so we don't have a repeat of Sunday."

"Just make sure they stay safe."

"They will." She looked over my shoulder and nodded. "Plus, there's protection."

I turned to see a male police officer come around the corner of the building into the car park. He gave us a wave.

"That's Gareth, I had a word with him earlier," she said quietly. "I know his mum and he was keen to tell me he thinks we're campaigning for the right thing."

"Well, that's something."

She touched my arm and smiled warmly. "It is. Now go and do your thing. I'll see you in there."

"Please be careful, Maureen."

A large black Mercedes was parked in one of the senior faculty spaces near the front entrance to the administration block. Glover's security man was leaning against the car, smoking a cigarette and watching me as I walked towards him. He had a few grazes and scratches on his forehead and nose, his lip was cut and there was a bruise over one puffy cheek. His left eye was black.

"Can I help you?" he asked.

I held up my lanyard. "I could ask you the same thing. You're not faculty."

"Not quite," he acknowledged with a tight, humourless smile.

"You look like you've been in the wars."

"Uh-huh." He inhaled deeply on his cigarette. "One of the perks of the job."

"Was it worth it?"

He shrugged and tilted his head back to blow a plume of smoke towards the sky. "You'd have to ask my boss that."

"I take it this is his car?"

"It is." He tapped on the rear window and I heard the soft whirr of a motor. "Councillor Morgan's here," he said.

The back door opened and Glover got out. He gave me a queasy smile, like he wasn't quite sure how to do it, and then walked around the back of the car.

"Councillor Morgan." He wore the dark trousers and waistcoat of an expensive-looking suit along with a white shirt, the crisp collar open. "It's good to see you." He held out his hand and I shook it. "No hard feelings, I hope, bearing in mind we seem to be on opposite sides of the fence here."

"None from me. I enjoy a healthy debate."

"Good." He rubbed his hands together as if he hadn't enjoyed shaking mine. "You're early for the meeting."

"As are you, unless you're here to lobby my colleagues as they go in?"

He looked at me in mock surprise. "Why would I need to, when I'm trying to put together a development that will help the people of this fine town?" It felt like he wanted me to bite, so I didn't say anything. He smiled slyly. "Surely that's what you want, too, isn't it, Councillor Morgan?"

"I want what I think is for the best, Mr Glover, but that doesn't include building on marshland and causing environmental damage."

"Which is your opinion."

"Yes," I said, "based on scientific data."

He conceded that point with a subtle nod of the head. "And yet others have a strop about it and we end up with violence in a public meeting."

"And you know that had nothing to do with Maureen."

"But do I?" he asked and glanced at his security guard. "Look at poor Tony. He was only trying to stop things from escalating and he got beaten up."

"Tony has my sympathy." It was all I could say, since I couldn't prove otherwise.

"I'm sure that makes him feel a lot better. Now is there any assurance I could give you to change your mind and vote?"

"There isn't, though I have to say having your employee follow me for a week didn't exactly endear me to your cause."

"Eh?" Glover frowned and looked wrong-footed for the first time. "Which employee is that?"

"Simon Ogilvy. I don't mind being approached, because that goes with the role, but I do object to being stalked and harassed."

He tapped his chin with a well-manicured finger. "That doesn't sound much like the Si Ogilvy I know, I have to say. As it is, my hands are tied. I granted him a leave of absence a fortnight ago and haven't seen him since."

My patience was wearing thin. "You have an answer for everything, don't you?"

"Quite often." He looked like he was enjoying himself.

"But I think I get to you, don't I?"

It was subtle but his expression hardened, ever so slightly. "Not at all."

"When was the last time someone said no to you?"

"It doesn't happen often," he acknowledged with a slight tip of his head. "Is that what this is to you? Are you flexing your muscles to make a point by denying me from doing good work for the community?"

Be professional, I reminded myself. "Even if you were proposing the golf course for the most altruistic of reasons, the majority of people in Seagrave won't be able to afford it."

"But some will," he said innocently. "Isn't that enough?"

"Not for the level of destruction to the marshland, no."

He pressed his hands together as if in prayer and put his index fingers against his lips. Tony lit another cigarette as he watched us without expression.

"Is it about the marshland?" Glover asked. "Or is it that you see me as a big fish and don't want that big fish to get any fatter?"

"Not at all. I understand capitalism and I also see that some people want to accumulate more money than they could ever spend, but that's not the case here."

"It's not that you're annoyed this could make a lot of money for me and my investors?"

I thought about Caitlin and the early-bird package. "No."

He glanced over his shoulder. "What do you reckon, Tony? Is she worried about money?"

"I don't know, boss," said Tony.

Glover faced me. "He likes to keep his own counsel and I appreciate that." He leaned closer. "Let me tell you this. I do want to develop the golf course and make a lot of money but here's the thing. Even if you and your little crusty band of protestors manage to block the plans, I wouldn't care."

That took me by surprise. "You wouldn't?"

"Why should I? I know you're an academic, so I assume you know what grants are?"

"I do."

"I will, of course, deny every word of this should you choose to repeat it elsewhere and Tony will be my witness, but I have high friends in low places who are smarter than the three of us combined." He tapped his lip again. "If you develop projects of benefit to the community and know how to apply, then there is a huge pool of funding available."

It suddenly made sense and I felt a spark of anger. I didn't hide it well enough because he smiled the smile of a predator going for the kill.

"I said you were smart, Kim, and I was right. You've got it, haven't you? The golf course itself is on the marshes you're so worried about but that won't be the money-making area. That's the hotel, you see, and since it's on a brownfield site, there's no problem. It could service a mountain biking track, or a nature reserve, or whatever I could get away with. You're hung up on the details when you need to follow the money. Even if I only build the hotel, which is a lot of profit, I still have the grant money. Me and my City backers are protected so the only people your protest would affect are local investors who are putting up their nest eggs and life savings. Whatever you do, I'm golden."

I felt nauseous. It was all a con. He'd had us running in all directions trying to save the marshes and he was ready to do an about-face and leave Caitlin and the other early-bird investors in the dust. "You're a nasty little man."

He shrugged theatrically. "Insults often mean someone has been bested, Kim, did you know that? But to make you feel better, I'll sit tonight in my very nice house overlooking Seagrave, with stables and a games room and lots of land and ponder on how I'm nasty."

"This was all a game to you, wasn't it?"

"Absolutely not. I genuinely like the idea of having my own golf course and what the fuck does anyone care about the marshes? When was the last time you went there? And if it's wildlife, could you even describe a wart-encrusted web warbler? No, you're doing this for a principle like I'm doing it for a principle but, right now, I'm better at it than you are. That won't always be the case, but it is now."

The fact he was right only frustrated me all the more. I had to walk away before I said something I would regret, so I turned on my heel and stalked towards the doors. My breath was hot in my throat and lungs as I pressed my pass against the reader and then I was into the empty foyer. I leaned on the desk and took a few moments to calm down.

Chapter 34

"Is everything okay, Kim?"

Startled, I turned as Colin, one of the friendlier campus security guards, came into the foyer carrying a couple of signs.

"Yeah, I'm just psyching myself up for the meeting, that's all. And Brian Glover caught me before I got in here."

"Ah, that would wear anyone down." He smiled broadly and his teeth glowed against his dark skin. "You're a bit early for the meeting, though, aren't you? I've only just started putting out the signs." He held one up. It was shaped like an arrow and had 'Council meeting this way' printed on it.

"Just a bit of prep work," I said. "Are there any students left on site?"

"A few in the library and a couple of tutorials were winding up as I came through."

"Fair enough. I'll leave you to your signage."

"Cheers," he said and stuck up a thumb. "Good luck with the vote."

"Thanks, Colin."

I crossed the foyer to the corridor, thinking about what Glover had said about Ogilvy. I doubted I'd be able to tell if the man was lying, but what if he was telling the truth? In that case, what was Ogilvy's agenda? Had my initial instinct about Ryan's photograph been right, that he and Caitlin were planning something together? Did she know Glover was prepared to let the early-bird investors down and viewed them as little more than collateral damage? Would that make her so desperate about my vote that she'd hire Ogilvy to harass me? If only I knew who the other person was that they were talking to. Had that person been involved? It surely couldn't have been Glover, because I'd seen him come in, but could it have been someone else from his organisation?

It felt like I was getting further away from understanding with every new piece of information that came my way.

I passed one of Colin's signs at the bottom of the stairs. I went up and three young women came around the dogleg, all wearing backpacks. I nodded at the two I knew, and one said "Hi, Kim" as they went by. I wondered if they were part of Adam's tutorial group.

Another sign pointed along the corridor to the humanities block as I walked by the main admin office. Movement caught my eye and I saw Adam walking between the desks. I was tempted to tap on the glass but didn't want to startle him. He stopped at the pigeonholes and took an envelope out of one tray and, although I couldn't be sure at this distance, it looked like he'd reached into mine. He turned the envelope over in his hands and tapped it a couple of times. Was he going to open my letter? I'd have been very surprised if he had done and, although it felt horribly voyeuristic, I couldn't look away. He tapped the end of the envelope then put his briefcase flat, opened it and dropped the letter in.

I felt terrible for thinking he was going to read my mail when he was obviously collecting it for me as I was off campus for the week. My paranoia was now making me suspect a friend who was being helpful.

There was a footstep behind me, and I turned to see Ogilvy step up off the staircase. He grinned broadly at me and moved his hand in a mock salute. A chill brushed my shoulders as we regarded one another for a moment or two.

"Evening, Kim. You know, for a councillor, you're a difficult lady to pin down."

Fear made my skin prickle and I felt horribly alone and vulnerable, even though Adam was in the next office. "Evening." I managed to keep my voice steady so as not to show how scared I was.

"I take it you're here for the vote?"

"Of course."

He took a step and so did I, maintaining our distance.

"We still haven't managed that conversation you promised me last Sunday, despite your obligation to the voters of this town." He smiled and took another step. "I wonder if I could report you for dereliction of duty?"

"Probably not." I stepped back. He knew we were in a public space and that if I made enough of a commotion someone would hear, so why was he doing this?

My trainer squeaked against the floor tile and I had a sudden thought. If I ran, my shoes would grip but his brogues probably wouldn't.

We matched another step.

"I just want to talk to you, Kim. Isn't that a reasonable request?"

Was that how he'd started a conversation with Freddy that fateful night? Had he been friendly to lull the younger man into a false sense of security or just gone straight for the attack? "Do you often make a reasonable request to talk like this?"

"Oh no, just with people I like."

"And what about with people you don't like?"

He shrugged, still smiling. "Life's too short to associate with people you don't like."

"What about students like Freddy Medwin?" I said and Ogilvy's smile faded a little. "You knew him, didn't you?"

"Nope."

We both took another step, and I glanced over my shoulder. There was a door about twenty feet behind me that led into the humanities block where the tutor offices were. If I could get into there, I might have a chance of getting away since he wouldn't know the layout.

"Yeah, you do. He's been all over the news and I saw your car parked very close to the pier on the night he was attacked." It was a shot in the dark, but I had nothing to lose.

His grin became predatory, and he stepped on a piece of grit that crunched under his sole. "I heard you'd seen something like that. Well, you know, sometimes people can make mistakes."

"Is that right?"

"Yes," he said and came at me in a sprint.

Chapter 35

Startled, I pushed off, too. He slipped, giving me a little head start. I'm not a runner but adrenalin warmed my muscles, and I took as big a stride as I could. The door was tantalisingly close.

His footsteps were hard and fast. I willed my legs to move quicker.

"Come here!" he shouted.

I propelled myself through the door hard enough that it clattered off the wall. I stumbled into the corridor and kept running.

"Fuck!" Ogilvy shouted. There was a heavy thud and I hoped he'd fallen and hurt himself.

I ran along the corridor. Adam's office was further down, and I could try and hide in there. Failing that, I could make it to the stairwell then head down to the foyer and get out.

The door banged behind me and I had to fight the urge to look over my shoulder. I knew Ogilvy was coming but if I saw him I'd be terrified, and I needed to keep thinking straight.

His breathing was loud and laboured. I tried to shut the sound out and focus on where I was running. There was a corner ahead, less than a dozen feet away. I pushed on as hard as I could and went into the corner with an almost perfect racing line, my shoulder barely grazing the wall.

The next corridor opened out. The stairwell seemed an impossibly long way away, but my heart soared as I saw Adam going into his office, his back and the edge of his briefcase showing. I didn't shout at him but pushed myself harder, closing the distance between us. If I could reach his room before Ogilvy turned the corner, then he wouldn't know where I'd gone and that would give me some breathing space to figure out my next move. My body protested and I couldn't seem to regulate my breathing.

I angled myself to run at the door and slapped at the handle. It opened and I ran through, stopping almost dead and ignoring the jarring in my legs to push the door closed quietly. I leaned against it, chest heaving.

Adam stood by his desk and looked at me open-mouthed. I put a finger to my lips and tried to suck air into my protesting lungs as quietly as possible.

"Bloody hell, Kim, what's going on? You sound like you're dying."

It seemed like he was shouting, and I held my hands out to shush him. "Please," I gasped. "Please be quiet."

"What…?"

I shook my head, my hands still out. He stopped talking.

"We need to be quiet," I whispered. It sounded horribly loud so I moved closer to the desk.

"Why?" he whispered back. "What's going on?"

"I'm being chased." I leaned on his desk. "That man, Ogilvy, is here."

"In the building?"

"Yes. I came in early for the meeting and saw you in the office and then he chased me."

"You saw me in the office?" He shook his head as if that didn't make any sense to him. "Why didn't you come in?"

"You were at the pigeonholes and I didn't want to bang on the window and scare you. When he charged at me, I ran."

"You must be terrified." Adam glanced at the door. "Where is he now?"

"He slipped and I managed to get a bit ahead but he's coming."

"Did he see you come in here?"

"I don't think so."

"Let me lock the door then," Adam said, "to give us a bit of time to figure out what to do. Did he say what he wanted?"

"Just that he wanted to speak to me, like before."

"Okay." Adam held up a hand in a calming gesture and took some keys carefully from his pocket then walked to the door. He rested an ear against it. "I can hear someone out there breathing heavily."

"So lock it."

"Yeah," he said and pulled the door open.

"What're you doing?" I demanded, my voice rising with fear.

Chapter 36

Adam stepped into the corridor.

"She's in here, you fucking idiot," he said then came back into his office and shrugged.

"Adam?" How could I have been so wrong about him?

He walked by me without speaking and stood behind his desk.

Ogilvy appeared in the doorway and smiled broadly. "Nice move, Kim," he said, breathing heavily. "You took me by surprise."

"You're not the only one," I said and glared at Adam. "What the fuck is going on?"

His smile was full of warmth. "Didn't you know? Oh, I'm sorry. Maybe I told you and you didn't listen because you were so completely self-absorbed, or maybe I didn't tell you because I didn't want you to fucking know." He made a weighing motion with his hands. "Hard to remember which it was, to be honest."

A pain started in my left armpit and rippled across my chest. I felt horribly disorientated.

"Get in here," Adam barked at Ogilvy. "I don't want anyone to see you."

"There's nobody here, mate."

"But there will be."

Ogilvy closed the door behind him and locked it. "There," he said. "All in it together."

Adam smiled at me like a benevolent uncle. "Feeling at a loss?" There was nothing malicious in his tone and he sounded almost amused.

"Yes," I said. I'd never felt more so. My mobile chimed with a text.

"You'd best ignore that, or Si will have to break your arm."

"I'll ignore it." I wished there was some way I could get my phone out of my bag without being seen, but that wasn't going to happen.

"I suppose all of this is a lot for you to process," Adam said, "though it's mainly your fault. Like everything else."

"Yeah," said Ogilvy. He leaned against the desk in front of me and folded his arms. "And you could have been more polite and had a chat when I asked."

"I saw Glover when I came in." My voice sounded like it was coming from someone else. "He said you aren't working for him."

"Well, it's good for me you didn't do your homework earlier," Ogilvy said.

"Pity you didn't shut her down earlier," Adam muttered. "Especially since her granddad's now gone to the police with some footage of you at the pier."

"What do you mean, shut me down, Adam?" I demanded. "Why would he want to do that?"

"Things haven't been done that should have been," Adam said. He went to check the door was locked. "Other things should have been dealt with before they became a problem."

He moved his arm as if he was throwing something and I heard a horrible, heavy crack.

Ogilvy looked startled and his eyelids fluttered. He made a throaty sound then his eyes closed and his legs folded. His head bounced off the desk as he fell.

Chapter 37

The round glass paperweight Adam held had a dark red smear on it. I put my hands to my mouth and wanted to scream but no sound came out.

"That's one issue down." He sounded calm but looked rattled. "And don't think about screaming because I'll smash your face in before you can start." He said it quietly and with conviction and I believed him.

"What are you doing? Why did you hit him?"

He shook his head with disappointment. "I'm trying to clear up so many loose ends it would make your head hurt."

"Aren't you even going to check him? He hit his head and there's blood on that paperweight."

Adam turned it in his hand and some of the blood smeared over his palm. "Shit," he said and walked around his desk. He sat heavily in the chair. "No, I'm not, because if he moves, I'll have to do something about it and that'll just be another fucking problem to deal with." He slammed the paperweight down hard. "I've been trying to make things right almost from the very bloody start. You didn't act like you were supposed to, Ogilvy was a dead loss and even Freddy backtracked on what he promised."

Hearing him say Freddy's name felt like he'd pinched me hard. "What does that mean?" Is this what Freddy had meant about me not knowing the full story?

"He was as much of a loser as bloody Ogilvy turned out to be."

Was I right about this being some kind of honeytrap? The fact Adam was telling me only muddied the waters I was trying to see through, because what did he have to do with the golf course? It felt like I was stuck in the middle of a situation that got more complicated with every moment. My eyes prickled with tears. "I don't understand, Adam."

"I don't understand," he repeated, cruelly mimicking my voice as he wiped his hand on a tissue. "How can you not see it?"

I palmed a stray tear away roughly. "Because it sounds like everything that's happened this week is down to you. Was it? Did you have one of those early-bird packages?"

He laughed. "You're comedy gold, Kim, I'll give you that. This hasn't got anything to do with the pissing golf course because, apart from you, who gives a flying fuck? This is about you being a bitch."

"A bitch?" It was like he'd thrown cold water at me and shocked away some of my disorientation. I felt my temper rise and gave into it. He was toying with me and I didn't like it. "Is that why you brained Ogilvy? You were the one who opened the door for him."

"Of course," he said and looked happy. "Now you're getting it."

"It sounds like you've gone nuts."

He leaned back in his chair and gazed at me as if he wanted to see into my soul. "Nuts, eh? Speaking of which, I loved you, did you know that?"

"Yes, I did. You told me a lot and I loved you, too."

"But not enough, eh?"

"No," I said with a slight shake of my head. "Not enough."

"I loved you like I'd never loved anyone else and that's why I knew we had something special."

"We split up, Adam, because we were better as friends."

"You decided to split us up, Kim. It was a terrible decision, but you'd made up your mind and, like the bitch you are, you had to get your way. I stayed friends because I thought I could make you see we were perfect for one another, but that never happened."

"I never forced you to get my own way." The decision had been hard to come to and certainly wasn't a whim.

"How is us splitting up against my wishes not you forcing me to do something?"

"We talked it through."

"And I said I didn't want it."

"It wasn't working for me. Did you want me to live a lie? That wouldn't be fair to either of us."

"I could have lived with it," he said. "Why couldn't you?"

"Why should I?" I thought back to those times when things weren't right, because our age gap got in the way, or we didn't do something because he'd already experienced it. Back then, he'd laughed away my concerns.

"Because a bit of compromise could have made us work perfectly."

"Compromise by whom?" Who did he think he was?

"By both of us." He said it matter-of-factly, as if it should have been obvious to me.

"I don't know what you want me to say."

"I don't want you to say anything, Kim, because I'm sick to death of you and I got what I wanted."

"What does that even mean?"

"Wow," he said. "You're slower on the uptake than I thought you would be."

I was fed up with his blustering. "So, tell me what's going on then. What did you do to Freddy?"

"He had one job to do and, from what I saw, he did a fucking good job. Excuse the pun."

I cringed but didn't say anything.

"Then the little bastard got a conscience."

I suddenly felt terribly cold. How had I fallen so completely for all of this? "It really was you, wasn't it? You hired those thugs and arranged for Freddy to rescue me."

He gave me a slow handclap. "Well done, Miss Marple. It's only taken you a week."

"Did you pay Freddy to take me to the garage and seduce me, too?"

"Seduce you?" He laughed sourly. "From what I saw of the footage, you couldn't get enough of him."

I shuddered at the thought of him watching. "You're sick."

Adam ignored me. "That's all he had to do. But then he came to me and said he'd made a big mistake. He hadn't realised you were a tutor and felt awful, because he'd fallen for you. Can you believe that? I hired him as a fucking rent boy and he fell in love. I said if he didn't keep his mouth shut, I'd let the police know all about it because there was nothing to link me and him."

"Did you have him killed, then? That was Ogilvy's car in the footage Pops shot, wasn't it?"

"It was. I borrowed his Mini because you'd be the only one who could make the connection and if the police somehow told you about it, you'd be too compromised to say anything. I didn't realise Pops would film it."

Fear crawled over me like a dozen spiders. "*You* attacked Freddy?"

"I hadn't planned to, and if he'd kept his mouth shut, I wouldn't have."

"But why kill him?"

"Because he wanted to make sure you knew the truth and told me he wrote a letter."

"I never got one."

He carried on as if I hadn't spoken. "He said he put everything in it about why I hired him. He knew Ogilvy was involved, and Caitlin."

"She was in on this?"

Adam held his hand flat and rocked it from side to side. "She didn't know about Freddy, but she was perfectly happy to get behind me destroying you." He smiled. "She hates you, in case you hadn't guessed. I've known her for years and she's a vindictive cow. She hated that you were younger, prettier and smarter than her."

All this deceit felt like I was being pelted. "I didn't know any of that."

"And there you go again, making yourself the victim. It's not a look you wear well."

"I'm not wearing a look."

"Yes, you are. You're as bad as Freddy was. He felt guilty and thought he could make up for his sins but made the mistake of telling me. I mean, did he expect me to pat him on the back and say, 'well done'? If you'd received that letter, then everything would've been out in the open and I wasn't going to let that happen. This was going to end with your life ruined and in the toilet, not mine."

I was angry now and the warmth behind my eyes was tears of frustration. "You killed him to ruin my life?"

"The fucker stood up to me. Can you believe that? He said he'd already sent the letter and then properly squared up to me, like he thought I was going to obey some Marquess of Queensberry rules."

"What did you do?"

"I had a stone in my hand and hit him as hard as I could. It only took one blow." He looked surprised. "I knew he wasn't getting back up from the way he dropped but I still checked his pulse, and he didn't have one, so I ran."

"Which is why he still had his wallet and watch. You panicked."

"What?"

"DS Richards knew he wasn't mugged because he still had his valuables on him. And she was right."

"And now she's never going to know."

"She will when I tell her," I said hotly.

He smiled sadly. "If you say so."

"You didn't have to kill him."

"In the end, it made it better, because then the police caused problems for you at work and that fitted into my plan perfectly." He shook his head. "All I wanted was to destroy you. I was already at the end of my tether, but the final straw was when we both put in for the head of department role. I told you I wanted it, but you couldn't even let me have that."

"That's not what happened," I said. "I put in for it first."

"No," he said vehemently. "Everything has to revolve around you, doesn't it, even if it means changing the narrative? I'd been able to keep a lid on my anger because I knew, at some point, there would be a way to get my revenge. But you putting in for the job was like you'd set me on fire and I couldn't take it anymore. I was sick to death of you getting your way and now, after breaking my heart, you were going to take my career, too? No fucking way."

"This is all because of that stupid job?"

"Are you even listening?" He was so furious he stumbled over the words. "You'd already taken away something I wanted, and you weren't going to do it again. You had to pay for hurting me, don't you see that? And once I stopped trying to curb my anger, it didn't take long to figure out how to hurt you. All I had to do was create a situation that smeared you forever and fucking a student did that. I knew you'd feel terrible and want to keep it a secret and when you did, I had you over a barrel."

"You wrote the notes, too?"

He laughed. "Yes, I enjoyed that. I knew you wouldn't go to the police, but I couldn't resist turning the knife a bit more."

"You're mad," I said. "And pathetic."

He stood up so quickly his chair clattered into the wall. "No, you're pathetic, because you're weak and couldn't figure this out. Freddy's pathetic because he couldn't finish the job he started." He strode around the desk and kicked Ogilvy's shoulder. Ogilvy groaned. "And he's pathetic, too."

"If only you could hear yourself," I said. I was so angry at him it was pushing back the fear and I looked at this big man and didn't want him to see me cower. "You're a weak, sad man who killed someone for a ridiculous reason."

Adam folded his arms and glared at me. "Who cares what you think? None of this is ever going to get out, Kim. Ogilvy won't say anything, even if I didn't brain him enough to do some damage, and Caitlin is scared of what this might do to her ambitions, so she'll keep her mouth shut."

"And are you going to keep me under lock and key until the letter arrives?" Another piece of the jigsaw fell into place. "You broke into my flat, didn't you? You had a spare key all the time." I shook my head. It was all so simple. "When you rang and I said I was out, you went to see if the letter had been delivered."

"That was your fault, too. You made the mistake of telling me about the footage, so I had to move things up a gear. That's why Ogilvy is here. I told him you were going to tell the police everything and that he needed to shut you up."

"But the letter wasn't at mine, was it?"

"And why would it be, when Freddy didn't know where you lived? But he knew where you worked."

The last part of the jigsaw fell into place. "He posted it to here, didn't he? It was in my pigeonhole."

"Now you're catching on."

"So, what now? People will notice if I'm not at the council meeting."

"Do you really think people will miss an obnoxious, local councillor who likes to cause aggro and has some kind of hard-on for everything Brian Glover is trying to do? I really doubt that. And what if they do?" He gestured around the office. "I have CCTV at home with video of you coming to my place and getting drunk and making a move. George is aware you have a drinking problem and there are plenty of witnesses who saw you and Freddy argue. I don't think it'd be a struggle to tempt a few to say they'd seen you acting unreasonably." He smiled. "I'm sure people saw you arrive but how hard do you think it'll be for an upstanding pillar of the community, like me, to persuade them you came into my office shouting the odds? Then, when Ogilvy came in, the pair of you started arguing because you'd met at the protest meeting and clearly didn't get on. He lunged for you, perhaps, or tried to hit you. You grabbed whatever you could and picked up the paperweight from my desk and brained him with it."

"Nobody will believe you," I said but even to me it all sounded frightening reasonable.

"Why not? You've hardly had a good track record this week, have you?"

"You're insane."

"And you're about to see your life collapse in front of your very eyes."

I pulled the briefcase towards me and hoped the letter was still in it.

"Leave that alone!"

I swung the case at him, and he stepped back out of range. I swung it the other way and it connected, with a crack, on his forearm. He yelped.

"Keep away from me, you psycho."

"Or what? What're you going to do?" He patted where his inside pocket would be on his sport coat. "You haven't got the letter."

I could see in his eyes he wasn't telling the truth. "Then I'll just use the case to get away."

"You can't keep swinging that all evening."

"I don't need to." I swung it with all my might at his head. He stumbled away but his feet got tangled with Ogilvy and he fell against the wall. I rushed to the door, unlocked it and pulled it open.

"Get back here, Kim!"

I ran towards the stairwell and had taken half a dozen strides before I heard him come out into the corridor.

"Kim!" Adam roared and then his pounding footsteps began.

Chapter 38

Adam was a big man, but he was fit and his stride was probably double mine. The briefcase didn't help and kept banging my leg but I didn't dare let go because then I'd have nothing to defend myself with.

The stairwell door was close enough for me to risk a glance over my shoulder. I shrieked when I saw he'd already narrowed the distance between us.

If he caught me before I reached the stairs there was nothing I could do. He could easily drag me back to his office and who would know? Maureen and Glover saw me come in, but would they raise the alarm straight away? Might they think I'd chickened out of the confrontation? Adam only needed a bit of luck and he could get me off campus and do whatever he needed to do to make sure I never told anyone what I now knew.

The thought of how much trouble I was in gave me a surge of energy. At the last moment, I planted my leg and pushed to the right, almost losing my balance. I stumbled and staggered through the stairwell door.

"Kim!" There was a thud, followed by a pained grunt and I assumed he'd stumbled as he tried to make the turn. His loss of momentum wouldn't give me much time, but it was enough.

I started down the concrete steps, concentrating so I didn't put a foot wrong. I'd reached the half landing before he came through the door. I held onto the banister with my free hand to stop myself from falling and looked up. His cheeks were red with exertion and I'd never seen him angrier. There was a mark on his forehead that looked like he'd cracked it on the door frame.

I went down the steps two at a time and was close to the ground-floor landing when something hit me hard in the small of my back. The force of the blow shifted my centre of balance and I reached for the banister but missed. I fell six risers and landed awkwardly, dropping to my knees and jarring them hard. I put out my hands to protect myself and the briefcase slid away.

Adam landed on his side almost beside me with a heavy thump. His breath woofed out and he curled up, hands across his belly. He'd brought me down but paid the price.

I scrambled to my feet, but my ankle gave way and I fell, my knees protesting at the fresh pain. I crawled forward to grab the briefcase and pulled it open. Freddy's letter was there. I snatched it up and kept crawling.

I pushed the ground-floor doors, but they wouldn't move. Gingerly getting to my feet, I leaned against the glass, but the doors were clearly locked.

"Oh no." Fresh tears gathered behind my nose and eyes. Colin must have locked them on his rounds because nobody would come this far into the humanities block.

I groaned. Everything seemed to hurt and my mouth and throat were dry. Painful pins and needles nipped at my fingers and toes. My thoughts were all over the place and I didn't know what to do, except that I needed to get out of here. That meant I had to go back upstairs, even though I'd have to walk past him and it didn't feel like I had the energy left to fight.

Adam groaned as he moved and that spurred me on. It was better to try when he was on the floor than have him stand up and confront me again.

Keeping out of his reach, I edged my way to the first riser. He got onto all fours, gasping with pain and his breathing had a heavy, hollow sound to it. "No," he muttered.

My knees protested as I took the first two steps. Adam made a lot of noise and I glanced over my shoulder to see he was now on his feet, gripping the banister but doubled over. I gritted my teeth and kept going. His breathing was loud in the enclosed space and when his hand brushed my ankle I screamed. I kept moving, wincing with every step and tears ran down my cheeks.

When I reached the half landing, he pulled my ankle. I went flat but got my hands under me so I wasn't winded. I kicked out at him but then he was next to me and pulling me up roughly, his big hands under my arms. He threw me against the parapet and towered over me, spittle flecking his lips, his eyes full of hatred. Blood ran out of the cut on his forehead. He didn't look anything like the man I'd thought I knew and I wondered if this monster had been there all along, hidden in plain sight.

"You're a fucking pain," he said with contempt. His breathing didn't sound so laboured now.

"Let me go, you bastard." I didn't want him to see how scared I was as I tried to figure out my next move. I couldn't take him on because he was way bigger than me and I wasn't even sure I could run anymore because of whatever I'd done to my knees.

"Give me the letter," he said through gritted teeth.

He had his back to the stairs, and I knew that was my only way out of this. I had to shove him down them. "Fuck off," I said and braced my back against the parapet to push myself to my feet. My knees flared with pain, but I moved anyway.

"Stay down and give me the letter."

I had the envelope in my right hand and closed my fist around it. "No."

"I can force you."

"Maybe, but we're in a college and people are here. I'll make enough noise to raise the dead and you'll be finished. You'll go to prison for what you did to Freddy and you deserve it, you fucking monster."

"I'm not going to prison," he said but didn't sound convinced. "I'll take you back to your flat, put you in the bath and slit your wrists."

"Nobody will believe that."

"A lecturer fucking her student and then lying to the police about it? I'll take my chances."

"You're not taking me anywhere, Adam. I'm taking this letter to the police."

He shook his head. "Give me the letter, Kim. I'm more than ready to hurt you to get it."

His hand closed around my mouth, his fingers pressing into my jaw. Before I had a chance to bite, he clamped down and I couldn't breathe. Panic coursed through me. He leaned closer, eyes seeming to bore into me.

Starbursts flared across my line of vision and my lungs protested. I swung both arms against him, but the blows didn't seem to faze him. He grabbed my right breast then slid his hand down my arm. I clenched the envelope tighter in my fist. I punched him in the face and his head snapped around, but he didn't release his grip.

He pressed his hand into my face, and it felt like he was going to break bones. I had to blink away darkness, like a twitch in my eye. I clawed for him and dragged my nails across his cheek then did it again, angling my fingers in harder. I drew blood and he cried out and swatted my hand away.

My vision was darkening, and my lungs were burning.

"What the fuck is going on?"

Adam's grip loosened as he glanced behind him. I sucked in air and saw Ryan over his shoulder at the top of the stairs.

I scratched Adam's cheek again and caught his eye. He cried out and pulled back, letting go of my face. My head tipped forward with a disorientating rush that made me feel sick.

Ryan was coming down the stairs. He looked horribly confused.

"It's not what you think," Adam said and took a step back from me. "She came in here and attacked a colleague of mine then started on me. He's in my office in a bad way. I managed to run but she caught me."

"You were trying to kill her," Ryan said. "I saw you."

"He hit Ogilvy with a paperweight and killed Freddy." I shifted my weight and winced. My right knee felt like it had glass in it.

Ryan stepped onto the half landing. Adam made a growling sound deep in his throat and tackled him. Both men went down and Adam sprawled over him, pinning Ryan to the floor and raining blows on his head.

I limped over to them. Ryan was trying to defend himself, but he was no match and the sound of Adam's fists pounding him were horribly loud.

I grabbed two handfuls of Adam's hair and pulled back with as much energy as I could muster. He let out an anguished cry and moved with me. I staggered back, trying to keep my balance and grip.

He screamed and then my right knee gave. I fell against the banister, ripping out handfuls of his hair and his momentum carried him around me to the top of the stairs.

"You fucking bitch!"

I moved without thinking and pushed away from the banister, stumbling into his stomach. The impact made him grunt and I slid to the floor, knowing I was done now.

His arms windmilled and his expression went slack when he knew gravity was against him.

Adam fell. I heard him hit the ground and then it was quiet.

Chapter 39

I sat beside Ryan on the step as he rang the police. His left eye socket was so bruised it was almost puffed closed, but he said he was okay. I stretched my right leg out because it was the only position that didn't make my knee feel like it was on fire.

I started shouting for Colin then.

Both of us watched the other flight of stairs as if expecting to see Adam crawl towards us but he didn't. Ryan checked him after helping me up and found he was still breathing but one of his legs was clearly broken and there was a lot of blood on his face. I admitted that was from me clawing at him as I tried to stop him crushing my skull.

"I should have got here earlier," Ryan said. He sounded tired.

"I'm lucky you came at all." I shuddered. The thought of what might have happened if he hadn't was terrifying.

"When you didn't reply to my text I came over. I reran the software with Adam's details, and he was the third person in that photograph of Ogilvy and Caitlin." He patted my hand clumsily. "There was no one in the conference room, so I worked my way back and heard you."

"I'm glad you did. He was going to kill me."

"You're safe now. You finished him off and you saved me."

We traded weak smiles and then I shouted for Colin again. Ryan joined in and we kept shouting until Colin appeared at the top of the stairs.

"What the bloody hell's going on?" he demanded. "What are you two raising merry hell for?"

As soon as he saw my face, he rushed down the stairs with a horrified expression. He squatted in front of me.

"What happened, Kim? Did you fall down the stairs? Have you rung an ambulance?" He looked at Ryan, as if seeing him for the first time. "Did she fall?"

"No," I said. "Adam attacked me."

"Adam?" Colin rocked on his heels. "But I thought you were a couple."

"We were," I said. "I don't think he took our break-up very well."

"Where is he?"

I pointed down the stairs and, with a frown, Colin looked. "Fuck me," he said and rushed down. He came back a few moments later with his mobile phone in his hand. "Did you ring an ambulance?"

"The police," Ryan said. "They're sending people."

"Adam's leg is proper busted up," said Colin.

"Good," I said. "The bastard deserved it. He also attacked the bloke in his office."

Colin looked as if he'd had a mild shock. "What?"

"It's a long story," I said and pressed the crumpled envelope from Freddy against my thigh. "It might take me a while to explain it to the police."

Acknowledgements

Mum, Sarah, Chris, Lucy and Milly; Nick Duncan, Sue Moorcroft, Julia Roberts, Jonathan Litchfield, Caroline Lake, Laura Burton and Helen Welch (whose honesty I needed); Steve Bacon and Wayne Parkin; Peter Mark May and Richard Farren Barber; The Crusty Exterior; my Con family; Priya Sharma and Tracy Fahey, for the massive confidence boost at Edge-Lit; Ian Whates and the NSFWG gang; Ross Warren, Jim Mcleod and Penny Jones, who continue to lead the charge; everyone who's bought, read and reviewed one of my books; the entire team at The Book Folks.

David Roberts and Pippa, for the Friday Night walks and other various adventures (and to the memory of Beryl Roberts).

Alison and Matthew, who make everything worthwhile.

If you enjoyed this book, please let others know by leaving a quick review on Amazon. Also, if you spot anything untoward in the paperback, get in touch. We strive for the best quality and appreciate reader feedback.

editor@thebookfolks.com

www.thebookfolks.com

Also by Mark West

All FREE with Kindle Unlimited and available in paperback!

DON'T GO BACK

Beth's partner Nick can't quite understand why she acts so strangely when they return to her hometown for the funeral of a once-close friend. But she hasn't told him everything about her past. Memories of one terrible summer will come flooding back to her. And with them, violence and revenge.

ONLY WATCHING YOU

After separating from her cheating husband, Claire begins to feel watched. She nearly gets run over and someone daubs a hangman symbol on a wall near her house. As letters begin to get added to the game, she'll need to find the identity of her stalker before they raise the stakes.

THE HUNTER'S QUARRY

Young single mother Rachel has no idea why an assassin is trying to kill her. Have they confused her with someone else? Did she do something wrong? Whatever the answer, it looks like they'll carry on trying unless she can get to safety or turn the tables on them. But first she'll have to find out what they want from her.

STILL WATERS RUN

A short holiday at the end of summer should be a chance for sixteen-year-old Dan and his recently divorced mother to unwind. Yet despite quickly striking up new friendships, their break takes a nasty turn when a holiday worker is murdered. Dan becomes embroiled in events. Can he get out or is he in too deep?

A KILLER AMONGST US

When her husband invites Jo on a couples' hiking weekend, despite disliking camping she accepts, hoping they'll rekindle their former closeness. But her hopes are shattered when the group starts to argue amongst themselves, and then the unthinkable happens… a happy holiday quickly turns into a desperate fight for survival.

Other titles of interest

WHICH CHILD by Shane Spyre

A disappearance, a bloody knife, a cruel murder. One of four identical sisters could be responsible. But they are protecting one another. Which child is the killer? And why did she do it?

FREE with Kindle Unlimited and available in paperback!

LIES WITHIN ME by Vanessa Garbin

After being taken speed-dating by her friends, Alice wakes up in a stranger's house. She can't remember the night before, but thinks she has been drugged and assaulted. Worse, however, is the man responsible is found murdered. Was it her? If not, who killed him? Finding the culprit might be the only way to get herself out of the frame.

FREE with Kindle Unlimited and available in paperback!

Sign up to our mailing list to find out about new releases and special offers!

www.thebookfolks.com

Printed in Great Britain
by Amazon

53605042R00111